S0-AJX-695

"Do you, Bradley Aaron Crawford, take this woman—"

Bradley Aaron Crawford? *Bradley Aaron Crawford!* Penny turned her head and myopically stared at the man standing beside her, the man that she was in the process of marrying. There was a small white bandage gleaming on his left temple.

Brad.

She never clearly remembered anything that happened during the rest of the ceremony. She must have made the right responses, since no one seemed to find anything out of the ordinary in the situation. Perhaps it was only her; obviously she was suffering from some sort of delusion, she decided, dazed. Although she'd been convinced she was engaged to Gregory Duncan, she was marrying Brad Crawford.

"I now pronounce you man and wife," Reverend Wilder intoned. "You may kiss the bride."

Slowly Penny turned to the man she'd just married. He carefully and tenderly lifted the veil from her face and folded it neatly back, then leaned down to kiss her.

"What are you doing here!" she whispered through barely moving lips.

He smiled and lightly kissed her on the mouth. "Marrying you."

Dear Reader:

The spirit of the Silhouette Romance Homecoming Celebration lives on as each month we bring you six books by continuing stars!

And we have a galaxy of stars planned for 1988. In the coming months, we're publishing romances by many of your favorite authors such as Annette Broadrick, Sondra Stanford and Brittany Young. Beginning in January, Debbie Macomber has written a trilogy designed to cure any midwinter blues. And that's not all—during the summer, Diana Palmer presents her most engaging heros and heroines in a trilogy that will be sure to capture your heart.

Your response to these authors and other authors of Silhouette Romances has served as a touchstone for us, and we're pleased to bring you more books with Silhouette's distinctive medley of charm, wit and—above all—romance.

I hope you enjoy this book and the many stories to come. Come home to romance—for always!

Sincerely,

Tara Hughes
Senior Editor
Silhouette Books

ANNETTE BROADRICK

That's What Friends Are For

Silhouette *Romance*

Published by Silhouette Books New York

America's Publisher of Contemporary Romance

For Faye—
A new friend, an old soul

SILHOUETTE BOOKS
300 E. 42nd St., New York, N.Y. 10017

Copyright © 1987 by Annette Broadrick

All rights reserved, including the right to reproduce
this book or portions thereof in any form whatsoever.
For information address Silhouette Books,
300 E. 42nd St., New York, N.Y. 10017

ISBN: 0-373-08544-3

First Silhouette Books printing December 1987

All the characters in this book are fictitious. Any
resemblance to actual persons, living or dead, is
purely coincidental.

SILHOUETTE, SILHOUETTE ROMANCE and colophon
are registered trademarks of the publisher.

America's Publisher of Contemporary Romance

Printed in the U.S.A.

Books by Annette Broadrick

Silhouette Romance

Circumstantial Evidence #329
Provocative Peril #359
Sound of Summer #412
Unheavenly Angel #442
Strange Enchantment #501
Mystery Lover #533
That's What Friends Are For #544

Silhouette Desire

Hunter's Prey #185
Bachelor Father #219
Hawk's Flight #242
Deceptions #272
Choices #283
Heat of the Night #314
Made in Heaven #336
Return to Yesterday #360
Adam's Story #367

ANNETTE BROADRICK

lives on the shores of The Lake of the Ozarks in Missouri, where she spends her time doing what she loves most—reading and writing romantic fiction. "For twenty-five years I lived in various large cities, working as a legal secretary, a very high-stress occupation. I never thought I was capable of making a career change at this point in my life, but thanks to Silhouette I am now able to write full-time in the peaceful surroundings that have turned my life into a dream come true."

IOWA

NEBRASKA

ILLINOIS

Payton

KANSAS

Kansas City

Missouri River

St. Louis

MISSOURI
Underlined places are fictitious.

ARKANSAS

Chapter One

A soft summer breeze gently caressed Penny's bikini-clad body. The muted sound of water lapping against the dock where she lay provided a rhythmic accompaniment to the periodic melodies of the birds who made their homes near the shores of Tawakoni Lake.

Penny Blackwell had always enjoyed summer and the opportunity to do nothing more strenuous than work on her tan. Being indolent made a pleasant contrast to the hectic schedule she followed the rest of the year.

She smiled to herself. In another week her usual summer routine would be changing permanently. The tempo of her life would doubtless be increased to the point where days like today would be very rare.

"That's a very secretive smile you're wearing these days, Runt," a deep male voice said from somewhere close by. "I find it quite provocative."

Penny's eyes flew open in shock, not only because she'd thought she was alone but also because that voice from her past should have been two thousand miles away.

"Brad!"

She was suddenly conscious of what a small portion of her body her bathing suit covered. Penny grabbed her matching cover-up robe, and with strangely uncoordinated movements for someone normally graceful, she pulled it on jerkily.

"What are you doing here?" After her first glimpse at the man towering above her, she refused to look up again.

Penny knew very well what Brad Crawford looked like. In that quick glance she'd seen that the only item of clothing he wore was a pair of faded cutoffs that should have been discarded years ago. They hung perilously low on his hips.

"Is that any greeting for a friend and neighbor whom you haven't seen in three years?" he asked. Without making an obvious effort, Brad leaned over and picked her up, placing her on her feet in front of him. Even with Penny standing, Brad continued to tower over her, the top of her head coming only to his collarbone. No one else had the ability to make her as aware of her lack of inches as Brad Crawford.

He slid his hand under her chin and lifted her face until he looked directly into her eyes. "You're looking even more beautiful than I remembered," he said, the warmth in his gaze adding heat to her already sun-kissed body, "and I didn't think I had forgotten anything about you." He paused, as though relearning every feature on her face. "I've really looked forward to seeing you again."

Penny's mind seemed to lose all discipline as thoughts she'd assumed were buried years ago flew around in her head like fragments of a jigsaw puzzle—the scraps indecipherable, creating a confusing mélange. She searched desperately through the hodgepodge of disconnected thoughts for something casual to say in response.

She could hardly parrot his last comment. She certainly had not looked forward to ever seeing Brad Crawford again.

"You surprised me," she replied in a feeble attempt to sound natural. "When did you get home?"

He glanced back to the shoreline where the two homes that had sat side by side for three generations overlooked the lake. "Not too long ago. I've been here long enough to find something to wear that is more in keeping with this Missouri weather," he said with a grin that was as familiar to Penny as her own. "I visited with Mom for a few minutes, but she knew I was eager to come find you, so she sent me off."

Penny fought to ignore the implication in that remark. Pretending that she no longer wished to sunbathe, she gathered up her towel and tanning lotion and started toward her home. Brad kept pace with her.

"Why are you here?" she asked, dreading his answer.

He confirmed her fear by answering, "I received an invitation to your wedding. I decided to come home to meet the knight who stole my princess while I was busy slaying dragons."

Penny fully intended to discuss Brad's invitation with her mother at the very first opportunity. Brad Crawford had definitely not been on the guest list Penny had prepared.

Keeping her eyes on the path in front of her, she grumbled, "I don't know why you always make everything sound so dramatic."

"Don't you, Penny? That surprises me. Seems to me drama comes easily for both of us."

That was true, but she resented being reminded. Why now, of all times? One week, that was all she'd needed. Then her life would be safe and secure, just as she planned. Not that Brad could possibly make any difference to those plans, but he did have an annoying habit of creating confusion and uncertainty in her life.

When she didn't answer him, Brad continued talking, sounding relaxed and companionable. "So tell me about him. The name was unfamiliar. Obviously he's not from Payton."

Penny felt a measure of safety as they drew closer to her home. She had no desire to carry on an intimate conversation with Brad. Once they reached the house she could depend on her mother to bridge any uncomfortable silences.

"Actually, Gregory moved to Payton from St. Louis a couple of years ago."

"What does he do?"

"He's an attorney."

"Ah," Brad responded as though some mystery had been solved for him. "An attorney," he repeated with satisfaction, "a nice, safe, unexciting profession."

She glanced at him with annoyance. "Not all of us crave excitement, you know."

"There was a time when you enjoyed it, as I recall."

"I was only a child. 'When I was a child, I used to speak as a child, think as a child, reason as a child; when I became a woman, I did away with childish things.'"

"My! Reverend Wilder would certainly be proud of you, remembering your Bible verses that way. Let's see, that's from the thirteenth chapter of First Corinthians."

"Your early training still shows, too, you know, otherwise you wouldn't have recognized it," Penny replied in an even tone. She pushed open the screen door to the enclosed porch with relief. "Mom? You'll never guess who's here," she called in a bright voice.

"Oh, yes I would," Helen Blackwell said. Her face beamed a welcome as she stepped out of the kitchen carrying a tray filled with cookies and a frosted pitcher of lemonade. "Brad checked with me to find out where you were." She set the tray down and hugged him. "Oh, it's just so good to see you again after all this time. What a marvelous surprise to everyone, having you show up so unexpectedly.''

Brad returned the hug with interest, his buoyant smile lighting up his face. ''I'm glad to see that someone is happy to see me,'' he complained good-naturedly, glancing at Penny out of the corner of his eye. ''For a moment there I thought Penny was going to shove me off the dock when she first saw me.''

''Don't be silly. You just startled me, that's all.'' Forcing herself to sound casual, she said, ''If you'll excuse me, I'm going to run upstairs and change.''

''Not on my account, I hope,'' Brad offered with an innocent grin. ''I'm thoroughly enjoying the view.''

Helen laughed. She would, Penny thought crossly. Her mother had always found Brad amusing. As far as her parents were concerned, Brad could do no wrong. He was the son they had never had.

A small voice inside her told her that, to be fair, she needed to remember that she had been the daughter Brad's parents had never had as well. Penny wasn't in the mood for fairness at the moment. ''If you'll excuse me,'' she said politely and left.

Helen poured lemonade in two of the glasses and said, ''Sit down, Brad. She probably won't be long. Why don't you tell me how things are going for you. I'm so eager to hear about New York and your life there. Everyone in Payton is so proud of you—the small-town boy who made good.''

Brad continued to stare at the door where Penny had disappeared.

''She's changed,'' he said in a flat voice.

Helen sighed. "Yes, she has," she admitted, "and in my opinion the change hasn't been an improvement."

Brad glanced at her in surprise.

Helen hastened to explain. "She seems to have lost some inner spark of enthusiasm, that enjoyment of life that always used to make her sparkle."

"I remember," Brad said with a smile.

"It could have been getting that teaching job as soon as she finished college. She wasn't all that much older than her high school students, which probably explains why she began to dress and act so much older than she really is."

"Does she like teaching?"

"Seems to. Of course, what she really enjoys is working with the drama club, directing their plays— she loves anything that has to do with acting."

"That isn't too surprising, since that's what she majored in at the university. She was one of the most talented students in our class. It's a shame she isn't using that talent now."

"I know. I suppose that's what bothers me about her. She seems to be settling for so much less than she's capable of."

"Such as Gregory Duncan?"

"Oh, heavens, no! Gregory is a brilliant man. Absolutely brilliant. He made quite a name for himself in the St. Louis area, I understand. Payton was extremely fortunate that a man like Gregory chose to move here and open a practice." Helen offered Brad the plate of cookies, pleased when he took a couple.

"Of course, he's extremely busy. He still has a considerable caseload in St. Louis, so he's been dividing his time between here and there. Penny's hoping his schedule will let up some once they're married."

Brad took a bite of one of the cookies and moaned his pleasure. "Sitting here eating your homemade oatmeal-raisin cookies certainly takes me back, Helen." After swallowing some lemonade, Brad returned to the subject of their conversation. "If Duncan's so well-known and established, he must be considerably older than Penny."

Helen nodded. "Yes, he is. He's thirty-nine, fourteen years older than she is."

"And she doesn't mind?"

"Doesn't seem to bother her in the least. Like I said, she acts so much older—seems so settled and all. You'd think they were much closer in age than they are." Helen reached over and took a cookie. "She seems to have her life all planned out now. Penny intends to continue teaching for a couple of years, then start a family. Gregory does a lot of entertaining. Just playing hostess for him will probably be a full-time job. She seems to be content with everything."

Brad gazed out through the screen that enclosed the large porch and murmured, "I wonder."

As soon as Penny returned downstairs, she could hear the animation in her mother's voice. Brad had that effect on people. He seemed to generate excitement wherever he went.

"Everyone in town watches *Hope for Tomorrow*," she heard Helen say, "wanting to see what outrageous things Drew Derek is going to do next. He's a real corker, isn't he?"

Brad laughed. "That he is."

"Of course I know you're nothing like him, but you sure make him out to be a real ladies' man."

Penny could hear the amusement in Brad's voice at her mother's careful phrasing when he replied, "Yes, he's certainly a real threat to the virtue of every woman he meets, isn't he?"

They laughed companionably. Penny decided it was time to join them and change the subject when she heard her mother say, "Well, I think you're just fantastic in the role and very believable. Why, if I didn't know the real you, I wouldn't let you anywhere near my daughter, that's for sure. Speaking of Penny, I taped your program on the video recorder every day during the school term so Penny could watch it when she got home. She—"

"Is there any lemonade left?" Penny asked, stepping out on the porch as though unaware she'd interrupted her mother. She could tell by the expression on his face that Brad had not been fooled.

"Of course there is," Helen answered. "You know I always keep plenty on hand in the summertime. It's our staple drink around here during these warm months."

"So you watch *Hope for Tomorrow* every day, do you?" Brad asked Penny, a half smile on his face.

Brad looked very much at home. His head rested on the back of the well-padded patio chair, his legs stretched out in front of him, crossed at the ankle. He held his glass balanced on his lean, muscled stomach.

Penny stepped over his legs and sank down in the chair on his other side.

"When I have the time," she responded casually. "Which reminds me. How did you manage to get time off to come home? If you really are here for the wedding, that must mean you plan to stay at least a week."

"What do you mean, if I'm really here for the wedding? Don't you believe me?"

She shrugged. "I don't disbelieve you. I just find it unusual that you'd bother."

"Oh, I don't, Penny," Helen said. "Why, Brad is the closest thing to a brother you've ever had. It's only natural he'd want to be here."

"That's very true. So I asked the powers that be in our production for the time and eventually they decided that Drew really did need some R and R from all of his bedroom activities." He watched Penny's profile while he talked because she refused to look his way. Instead, she stared out at the lake. Of course, it was a very relaxing view, but she was studying it as if she'd never seen it before. Glancing at Helen, seated on his other side, he continued, "So they've put poor old Drew in a coma for a few days."

"Oh, really?" Helen said. "What caused it?"

Brad shrugged his shoulders. "Who knows? Too much sex, probably."

"Brad," Helen said, laughing. "That's awful."

"Sorry," he said in a teasing tone that said he wasn't sorry at all.

How many times over the years had Penny heard that exact inflection in his voice? Somehow it had always managed to get him off the hook. Perhaps because when he was in that mood he was practically irresistible.

"Besides," he went on, "I felt I had to meet the man who stole Penny away from me."

Penny stiffened at his words, but before she could come up with a caustic reply she heard her mother say, "Well, then you should plan to come back over for dinner tonight. Gregory is going to be here. It will give the two of you a chance to visit together, sort of get acquainted and all before the wedding."

Oh, Mother, how could you? Penny silently pleaded. No two men could be more unalike than Gregory and Brad. The evening would be a total disaster. What in the world would they find to talk about?

"Why, Helen, thank you," Penny heard Brad say, and a definite sinking sensation developed in her stomach. "That would be great." He glanced at his watch. "In that case, I'd better get home so I can visit with Dad when he arrives. I'm sure they'll understand why I'm over here my first night at home."

Damn him. Why did he keep making those little remarks, implying a great deal more than he had reason to? When Helen accepted his comment with an understanding smile, Penny could have thrown something.

Which was exactly why she didn't want Brad Crawford anywhere around her.

Penny considered herself to be a calm, even-tempered person. Everyone at school commented on how well she handled her adolescent students. She did not get upset. She did not lose her temper. She was in control at all times. Brad was the only person who had ever caused her to lose that control, and Penny hated his ability to upset her. Absolutely detested it.

The past three years had been wonderfully serene, and she was looking forward to a lifetime of similar peace and serenity. In other words, she intended to spend her life anywhere that Brad Crawford wasn't.

Penny waited while Brad and Helen made arrangements for his return that evening, smiled politely when Brad said goodbye and watched as he left her home and sauntered across the immense lawn that separated their two places. Then she turned to Helen.

"Do you know anything about how Brad received a wedding invitation, Mother?"

Helen had just picked up the tray to return to the kitchen. She looked puzzled by the question. "I sent him one. Why do you ask?"

"Because his name wasn't on the list."

Helen went into the kitchen; Penny followed. "I knew it was just an oversight. After all, you sent one to his folks. So I just stuck one in the mail to him as well."

"It was no oversight."

Helen set the tray on the kitchen counter and turned around. "Penny! Are you saying that—you mean that you didn't intend for Brad to come to your wedding?'' Her shocked surprise could have been no less than if Helen had just heard that Penny was pregnant with triplets.

"That's exactly what I mean."

An expression of pain crossed Helen's face. "Oh, Penny. That's awful."

"What's awful about it, Mother? It's my wedding. I should be able to invite or not invite anyone I please."

"But to leave Brad out, after all you've meant to each other during these years."

"Mother, don't exaggerate. Brad and I grew up together because we lived next door to each other. Since we're almost five miles out of town, we didn't have too many choices as to whom we played with. And if you remember anything, you can certainly recall that we spent most of our time together fighting!"

Helen leaned against the counter, staring at her daughter as though she no longer knew her. "Why, Penny, that isn't true! Of course you squabbled at times—any kids who spent much time together would be likely to bicker. Besides, you're both extremely strong-willed and determined to get your own way. No one would expect that you'd always agree on everything."

Penny absently opened the pantry door and peered inside with absolutely no idea what she was looking for.

"But, Penny, the two of you were friends. Close friends. I don't understand your attitude toward him now."

Penny closed the door and turned around. "Well, I don't suppose it matters now, does it? He's here and he'll be here for dinner. I think I'll go on up and take a bath. I want to look calm and relaxed when Gregory gets here."

Helen stood and watched Penny as she went into the hallway and started up the stairs. There were times she didn't feel she understood her daughter at all.

Penny stared at her reflected image in the mirror. The pale peach of her dress showed off her darkening tan and brought out the red highlights in her russet-colored hair. She had pulled her hair smoothly away from her face into a cluster of curls at the nape of her neck. She looked poised, sophisticated and calm.

If only she felt that way! Her insides had been churning all afternoon, which was absolutely ridiculous. What possible difference could it make that Brad Crawford would be there for dinner? she asked herself.

Unfortunately she could come up with a half-dozen reasons before she had to draw breath. She knew him too well. Depending on his mood, he could be everything a hostess could want in a polite dinner guest. Or he could be perfectly outrageous. Funny, but outrageous. And he knew entirely too many things about her that he could bring up if he felt the urge. It wouldn't be the first time he'd embarrassed her in front of someone important.

"Oh, Mother," she lamented aloud, "If you'd only asked me, I would have told you that Brad's favorite pastime is ignoring the script and improvising in a situation." A reluctant smile played on her face when she thought of some of the things he'd done in the past. He really did have a wicked sense of humor.

She realized that she was being a coward, hovering upstairs when she'd heard him arrive at least fifteen minutes earlier. Penny had justified her delay to herself, knowing that her father would monopolize Brad for a while. Sooner or later she would have to face him. Glancing at her watch, she decided now was as good a time as any. Gregory should be arriving before much longer.

Sure enough, she found Brad and her father in animated conversation. They'd always gotten along well. Her dad had gone to all of Brad's Little League games and stood on the sidelines cheering during his high school football games.

The little voice inside her said, And don't forget, you were right there, cheering with the best of them.

Of course she was. She'd been proud of Brad. He was a natural athlete and she'd enjoyed seeing him play. But that was years ago, after all—just part of her childhood.

Brad stood up as soon as she walked into the room. "Wow!" he said in a reverent voice.

Penny couldn't help it. She began to laugh. "That's one of the things I've always liked about you, Brad," she said, grinning. "You were always so articulate, with such an artful turn of phrase."

He walked over to her and took both her hands, staring down at her. "And that laugh is one of the things I've always liked about you. I had almost given up hope that it was still around."

She could not ignore how well Brad looked in the navy blue blazer and gray slacks. The ensemble set off his blond good looks. Let's face it, she thought, he looked like every woman's dream of the man she hoped would appear in her life and take her away from daily drudgery. No doubt that was one of the reasons *Hope for Tomorrow* had become one of the most successful daily serials.

The doorbell served as a reprieve from Penny's runaway thoughts. "Oh, there's Gregory now," she said, unconsciously betraying her relief.

Brad frowned slightly as he watched her return to the hall. For just a moment he'd seen a glimpse of the Penny he'd known forever, but then she'd disappeared behind the polite, sedate facade of the woman he'd seen this afternoon.

He heard murmured voices in the hallway, and an intimate male chuckle that caused the hair on his neck to rise in protest. Brad determinedly ignored the fact that Penny's lipstick was definitely smudged when she returned to the room, leading a man who must have been Gregory Duncan.

Brad wasn't prepared for the shock he received when he saw Penny's fiancé. There was no denying that he was in his late thirties. The mark of time had

added character to his face. What hit Brad like a dou-
bled-up fist in his stomach was that Gregory Duncan
looked enough like him to be a close relative.

They were both approximately the same height and
build, and their hair was the same shade of blond.
Brad felt as though he were looking into the future, at
what he would look like in another thirteen years.

And this was the man Penny had chosen to marry.

After the introductions were made, Brad said, "I've
looked forward to meeting you, Gregory. I've heard
some very good things about you." He didn't miss the
exchange of glances between Gregory and Penny.

"It's good to meet a friend of Penny's, Brad,"
Gregory replied in a deep, mellow voice that Brad was
sure could be used to great effect in a courtroom.
"Unfortunately, I'm at a disadvantage. She's never
mentioned you to me."

Brad glanced at Penny in surprise, and acknowledged to himself the pain Gregory's remark caused
him. She had truly dismissed him from her life.

Penny couldn't meet Brad's eyes. She smiled at
Gregory and said, "Oh, I'm sure I told you about
Brad, Gregory. You've probably just forgotten. He
lived next door for years."

"I'm sure you have, love," Gregory said, holding
her possessively to his side. "It must have slipped my
mind."

Brad was unprepared for the almost despairing rage
that swept over him at the sight of Gregory holding
Penny so intimately.

What had he expected, for God's sake? She was marrying the man, wasn't she? He found himself clenching his teeth in an effort to control his emotions. Helen earned his undying gratitude when she came into the room and announced that dinner was ready.

Dinner was almost as bad. Brad sat across the table from the engaged couple, a silent witness to their smiles and murmurs. Ralph and Helen kept the conversation going, and Brad determinedly joined them, knowing he would have to deal with his pain later.

Penny began to relax about midway through dinner. As usual, her mother had outdone herself with the meal, and the men were obviously enjoying it. She had just felt the tension in the muscles along her spine ease when Brad said, "Too bad you never learned to cook like your mom, Runt. Maybe she'll take pity on Gregory and have you two for dinner often."

Gregory glanced up from his meal and looked at Brad in surprise. "What did you call her? Runt?"

Brad looked a little abashed. "Sorry. I guess that just slipped out. It was a nickname I gave her years ago."

Gregory's gaze fell on Penny. "I can think of many nicknames I might choose for her, but nothing so revolting as that."

"She was always small for her age, you know," Brad said lightly. "I think she always hoped she'd catch up with me, but by the time we were teenagers she knew she'd well and truly lost the race." He studied Penny for a moment, then smiled. "She's always looked younger than her years, anyway, don't you think so?''

Gregory smiled at her. "Oh, I don't know. I'd hardly confuse her with one of her students, despite her height. She's a very nicely endowed woman.''

"Thank you kindly, sir,'' she said.

"As for her cooking,'' Gregory went on, "Penny doesn't have to do anything she doesn't want to. I'm not marrying her to gain a housekeeper.''

"Of course not,'' Brad agreed. With a perfectly deadpan expression he went on, "I just hope you don't mind the fact that she snores.''

The reaction of those around the table was a study of mixed emotions. Ralph looked as though he were trying not to laugh while Helen looked shocked. From the expression on her face, Penny looked as if she could have easily committed murder. Only Gregory showed little reaction—just a slight narrowing of his eyes.

"I had no idea you knew Penny quite that well.''

"He's being obnoxious,'' Penny said heatedly. "Our families used to go camping together when we were children. Brad always used to accuse me of snoring, just to make me angry.''

"And it usually worked,'' he replied with a grin.

She struggled with her anger now, unwilling to let him know that he had succeeded in riling her once again. She tried to laugh, but wasn't sure that anyone was fooled. "But not now. Your childish tricks no longer have any effect on me.''

Brad leaned back in his chair. "That's good to know, Runt. That uncontrollable temper of yours used to get you into lots of trouble."

"Temper?" Gregory repeated, lifting a brow. "You must have Penny confused with someone else. A more even-tempered person I've yet to meet."

Brad began to laugh. "Oh, dear. Are you ever in for a surprise, Counselor." He leaned forward and rested his arms on the table in front of him. "How long have you and Penny known each other?"

"About a year, wouldn't you say?" Gregory answered, turning to Penny.

"Something like that," she muttered.

"And she's never lost her temper?"

"Not that I'm aware of."

"How very interesting," Brad mused.

"Only to you, Brad, dear," Penny said sarcastically. Then she stood and said with a smile, "I'll clear for you, Mother. Who would like some cherry-chocolate cake?" She refused to look at Brad.

No one could pass up such a temptation, so Penny carried the dishes into the kitchen and began to slice the cake and place it on plates. She glanced up when she heard the swinging door open, then frowned.

"You don't need to help, Brad. I can manage."

"I know. I just came in here to apologize."

"It's too late."

"Too late for what? Do you think he's going to beg off or something just because he's found out you have a temper, for God's sake?"

"I mean it's too late for you to think I'm going to always say, 'Oh, that's all right, Brad, it doesn't matter.' You think you can say anything you want, behave in the most outrageous manner, and all you have to do is smile that devastating, knee-weakening smile and I'll forgive you."

"Knee-weakening?"

Trust Brad to pick up on her unfortunate choice of words.

"A figure of speech, Brad, nothing more."

"Does my smile really affect you that way?"

"Would you get out of here?" She picked up two plates filled with cake and shoved them into his hands. "Make yourself useful."

Penny watched as Brad laughingly returned to the other room, looking for all the world as if the two of them had been out in the kitchen laughing over old times.

Something told her that the next week might have a certain lack of peace and serenity. She would count the days until the wedding.

Surely after she and Gregory were married, Brad Crawford would no longer have the ability to disrupt her life.

Penny refused to ask herself why this would be so.

Chapter Two

Good morning, Mr. Akin," Penny said the next morning. She placed the large package her mother wanted mailed in the window of the Payton post office and waited to have it weighed.

"Well, hello there, Penny," he replied. "Guess you're pretty busy these days, what with getting ready for your wedding and all."

She smiled at the elderly man who had worked at the post office as long as she could remember. "Yes, I have been."

"Did you know young Brad Crawford is back in town?" he asked, his intent gaze letting her know it was no idle question.

"Yes, I did. He had dinner with us last night, as a matter of fact."

"Did he now? That's right interesting, considering you're marrying somebody else."

"What difference does that make?"

"Well, folks around here kinda figured that sooner or later you and the Crawford boy would end up married to each other."

"I have no idea why they would think that, Mr. Akin, just because we were next-door neighbors for years."

"It's probably because the two of you were thicker than fleas on a hound's back, missy," he said in a no-nonsense voice. "Never saw one of you that the other one wasn't right there as well."

"That was a long time ago, Mr. Akin. We were just kids then."

"You weren't just kids when you went off to college together. Why, everybody knew that Brad spent his first year out of high school here in Payton, just waiting for you to graduate so you could go to school together."

"Mr. Akin, Brad worked at the textile mill for his dad the year after he graduated from high school. He was tired of school and wasn't sure what he wanted to do."

"Hmph. Figured that out quick enough when you decided to go up north to that big university to study acting, though, didn't he?"

Why was she debating the issue with a postal employee? People were going to think whatever they wanted to think, no matter how much she tried to explain. Penny managed a noncommittal response that seemed to appease him and watched as he weighed the package.

After paying him, Penny waved goodbye and went to the grocery store to pick up a few items her mother wanted. When she was ready to check out, she noticed Sonia Henderson had the shortest line of people waiting. She and Sonia had gone through school together, but instead of going to college, Sonia had married her high school sweetheart.

As soon as Penny began to unload her basket onto the moving belt, Sonia saw her.

"Penny! Did you hear that Brad Crawford is in town?"

Why did everyone want to tell her about Brad's visit, for Pete's sake? "As a matter of fact, I did, Sonia." Trying to forestall another interrogation, she asked, "So how are Timmy and Sarah?"

"Oh, they're fine. Timmy's glad to be out of school for the summer. Sarah's teething and she's been a little cranky, but Mom says that's only natural." Almost in the same breath she asked, "Have you seen him yet?"

"Seen who?"

"Brad! Have you seen him since he came back?"

"Uh, yes. I saw him yesterday."

"Does he look as good as he does on television?"

Better, Penny thought, but decided there was enough conjecture flitting around town without her adding to it. "About the same, I guess."

"Did he talk to you about what it's like, living in New York and being famous and everything?"

"Actually, no, he didn't."

"I think it's so exciting he's here. I hope I get to see him. Do you suppose his life is anything like Drew Derek's?"

"I have no idea."

Sonia giggled. "He probably wouldn't tell you if it was."

"Probably not," she agreed.

"Can't you just imagine what it's like, being famous and all, knowing all the women are dreaming about wanting to make love to you?"

Penny was saved from having to think up a reply when Sonia rang up the total for the groceries. Penny conscientiously concentrated on writing out her check. By the time she managed to get out of the grocery store, she was thankful her mother hadn't thought of any other errands for her to run. If one more person brought up Brad Crawford's name today...

"Good morning, Penny. I always thought that shade of yellow looked great on you."

Thank God she had a good grip on the two sacks of groceries. "Brad! Where did you come from?"

"Why, Penny, you never cease to amaze me. We had a discussion about the birds and the bees years ago. My, how quickly we forget."

"You're not funny, Brad. How long have you been lurking outside the grocery store?"

"I wasn't lurking. I happened to see your car parked out here when I drove by earlier and decided to see if you'd like to go get something cold and refreshing to drink with me."

"I need to get these groceries home," she explained with a certain amount of relief. Brad was looking every inch the virile male in his prime this morning, in faded jeans that fit him like a second skin and gave no doubt to his gender. The tan sport shirt he wore accented his well-developed shoulders and chest. His blond hair, worn much longer than most of the local men's, gleamed brightly in the morning sunlight.

"That's all right. I'll follow you home and we can go in my car."

She closed the trunk and came around to where he was casually leaning against her car. "Not today. I have too much to do."

"Such as?"

Penny quickly racked her brain, trying to think of something. What did she usually do on Saturdays? In the summertime? Not much. How about the Saturday before her wedding? Surely she had something urgent, something really vital, that could not be postponed another hour.

She couldn't think of a thing.

"Don't you want to have a drink with me?" he asked quietly.

Penny hadn't heard that note in his voice in a long time. It caught her totally off guard. She had heard pain, despite his attempt at lightness.

"It's not that, Brad," she began uncertainly.

"We haven't had a chance to talk since I got home, Penny," he reminded her, reaching out and touching a russet curl at her ear.

"Of course we have," she said, trying to defend herself. "We talked yesterday afternoon, then again last night."

"No, we didn't. You didn't say a half-dozen words around me yesterday, except for telling me off in the kitchen." He studied her in silence for a moment. "Are you still angry at me because of last night?"

Trying to ignore how close he was, she opened the car door and slid behind the steering wheel. After pulling the door shut, she looked up at him. That particular look in his eyes had always been able to sway her, even against her better judgment. And she was aware that she had overreacted to his teasing the night before. "All right," she said, giving up the struggle. "I'll see you at home, then."

His smile lit up his face, and for a moment she could only stare at him. He seemed to glow with it. No wonder he had been an instant hit on television. With that much charisma, he was lethal to a person's peace of mind. Or at least, to her's.

Brad followed her home and pulled into her parents' driveway directly behind her. He helped her carry the groceries into the house. "I'll be right back," he said as soon as he set one of the sacks down. "I'll meet you out front in a few minutes."

Penny hurriedly put the groceries away, found her mother working in the flower garden and told her that she was going out to have a drink with Brad.

"If Gregory should call, tell him I'll be home within the hour."

Helen glanced up at her absently. "I will, dear. Have a good time."

Have a good time. How often had her mother said that to her over the years? Probably every time she had taken off with Brad. Her mother had never seemed to worry about her as long as she and Brad were together.

Penny thought about her instructions to her mother for a moment. She didn't really expect Gregory to call. He'd been out of town all week and had told her last night he would probably have to work at the office all weekend. But they were going to have dinner together that night.

Penny smiled to herself as she walked through the house and out the front door, thinking about next week. They were going to take a week off for their honeymoon, although she had no idea where they were going. Gregory told her it was going to be a surprise. She really didn't care as long as she didn't have to compete for his attention with his law practice. For a few days, anyway, she would have him all to herself.

"There's that wicked smile again, Runt," Brad said, and she realized he'd already returned to his car and was waiting for her. "If I didn't know you better, I'd think the innocent Ms. Blackwell was thinking impure thoughts about something—or somebody."

She could feel the color mounting in her cheeks and cursed her fair complexion that let her reaction to his remark show. She knew from his grin that he hadn't missed her blush. "What makes you so sure I'm all that innocent, Brad?" she drawled. "After all, I'm twenty-five years old."

"Age has nothing to do with your innocence," he said with emphasis, holding the passenger door open for her.

He backed out of the driveway, and because she was so caught up in the conversation, Penny didn't notice that he had turned the opposite way from town when he got to the road.

"You don't know everything about me," she said emphatically. "After all, you haven't seen me in three years."

"So what? That doesn't mean I haven't kept up with what's been happening to you."

Penny turned so that she unconsciously fell into the familiar pose she'd always used whenever they went anywhere in the car together—she leaned against the door and pulled one knee up on the seat so that she was facing him.

He darted a lightning glance at her and immediately returned his gaze to the country road, a slight smile on his face.

"Your mother doesn't know everything I do," she said, irritated that she felt the need to defend herself.

"No, but yours does."

"Hah! Not likely." She was quiet for a moment, then asked, "Are you telling me that Mother has been writing to you?"

"Sometimes. Sometimes she just tells my mom, who passes along any relevant information."

"Which I'm sure you found very boring."

"You might be surprised."

They were quiet for a few minutes. Penny watched the passing countryside without registering that they were leaving Payton farther and farther behind. She was too busy trying to analyze what Brad was telling her.

"Then you knew all along when I started dating Gregory?"

"I knew," he agreed with a smile.

"If that's the case, then why did you ask last night?"

"Just being polite."

"That's a laugh," Penny said, although she didn't sound particularly amused. "You don't know the meaning of the word."

"Aah, Penny. I'm crushed. After I tried so hard."

"I know how hard you tried—to be irritating and aggravating."

"Did it work?"

"What do you mean?" she asked, straightening her back. "Do you think you bothered Gregory with your childish remarks? He's much too mature for that," she added, her tone sounding remarkably pleased.

"I'll say. He's almost old enough to be your father."

"He is not! He's only fourteen years older than I am," Penny responded heatedly, unaware that she and Brad had fallen once again into their age-old conversational pattern of baiting and fencing.

"Does he have any children?" Brad asked with polite interest.

"Since he's never been married, I rather doubt it," she replied with more than a little sarcasm.

"Or if he does, he probably doesn't talk about it," Brad added agreeably.

"Brad!"

"Sorry," he said with a grin, neither looking nor sounding particularly sorry. "So why is he getting married now?"

Penny could feel her temper getting the best of her, which only added to her irritation. How was it that Brad could set her off so quickly with his idiotic remarks? "You are really being insulting, you know that, don't you?" she said, her eyes frosty with disdain.

"Well, of course he loves you, Penny," Brad hastily assured her. "Who wouldn't? I just wonder what other reasons such a logical and analytical person might find to choose you for his mate, particularly since he's waited this long to marry."

Who wouldn't? Penny's mind repeated in surprise, losing much of what he had said after that. Was it possible that Brad had actually intended to pay her a compliment? If so, it was the first she could ever recall receiving from him.

"What other reasons could he have?" she asked, curious about his line of thinking.

"Oh, there are all kinds of reasons to get married. Maybe he's tired of living alone. Maybe he wants a family, a hostess. Maybe he's marrying you for your money...."

"That's a pretty vivid imagination you've got there, Brad. Do you write those stories on television as well as act in them?"

"There's nothing imaginative in any of that. It happens all the time."

"Not with me, it doesn't. I doubt that my teacher's salary attracts him. After all, he's a very successful lawyer."

"Then why did he move to Payton?"

Penny relaxed a little more against the door, watching Brad's profile. "Why not? It's a nice place to live, even though you found it dull."

"I never found it dull," he pointed out mildly. "I just wanted to become a professional actor, and Payton doesn't have that many job openings in that particular field." He glanced over at her and grinned when he saw that she was absently twisting a curl around one of her fingers. She only did that when she was agitated. Good. At least he had her thinking. "Besides," he went on blandly, "I wasn't talking about what you make. You're an only child and your family is very well off."

"So what? I'm certainly not apt to be inheriting anything for years to come, and you know it. Good grief. Mom and Dad are still in their forties."

"I know. They got married very young and they made it work but it was tough, which is why they're against teenage marriages."

Penny looked at him in surprise. "How do you know that?" she asked. "I've never heard them say anything about their early years."

"Never mind," he replied, deciding it was time to change the subject. "So if he isn't interested in your money, Gregory must want you to play hostess for him and preside over his home."

"What's wrong with that?" she asked, puzzled by his tone.

"Oh, Penny, that isn't you, and you know it. You've got too much vitality and sparkle for that kind of life. If you would just be honest with yourself, you'd admit that you're already bored with teaching school. How do you think you're going to feel playing helpful Harriet for a man who could pass as your father?"

"Would you stop with the stupid remarks about Gregory's age? In the first place, Gregory doesn't even look that old. As a matter of fact, you may have noticed that he looks a little like you—same hair coloring, similar build."

He grinned. "Is that why you fell for him? Because he reminded you of me?"

She stared at him in horror. "Of course not! He's absolutely nothing like you, thank God."

"You don't have to sound so thankful. I didn't turn out all that bad, did I?"

She heard the hint of pain in his voice again, and wondered about it. Brad Crawford was too self-confident to be easily offended. And yet twice today she had heard a slight hesitancy in his voice as though he were unsure of himself.

"You're living your life the way you want to, Brad. I can't fault you for that," she said quietly.

"But are you living your life the way you want to? That's my concern at the moment."

She glanced at him, puzzled. "That's the second time you've made a remark like that. I am not bored with teaching. I am very content with my life." She studied him for a moment in silence, then asked, "And why should you care what I do or how I feel, anyway?"

"Come on, Penny, you know me better than that. I have always looked out for you and cared for you, ever since we were kids." He gave her a quick glance from the corner of his eye and smiled. "Why should I stop now?"

She wasn't going to let that statement go unchallenged. "Yet you could hardly wait to leave here once you finished college."

He was quiet for a moment. He heard the hurt in her voice and realized once again what a fine actress she truly was. Until now he had never really known that she had cared when he'd decided to go to New York. An interesting discovery, considering how he'd felt when she had blithely greeted his news three years ago by wishing him well.

"You could have gone with me," he said finally.

The interior of the car seemed to reverberate with sudden emotion. The silence that fell between them seemed to grow like a living thing, until Brad felt that he could almost reach out and touch it. Whatever she was feeling, it wasn't indifference. That he knew. He wished he'd had this conversation with her then, instead of now. He'd paid for his cowardice every day since.

When she did speak, her anger surprised him. "Of course I could have gone. We could have starved together! Why would I have wanted to go to New York, Brad? I was twenty-two years old. It was time for us to grow up, accept responsibility, make something of ourselves. Playtime was over...at least it was for me."

"Is that all that acting was to you, Penny? Playtime?"

She laughed, but she didn't sound in the least amused. "Well, it certainly isn't a way to make a living."

"I haven't done so badly at it."

Penny felt a sudden urge to hit something, she felt so frustrated. Who was she kidding, anyway? Why didn't she just admit the truth?

"Actually," she said, wishing her voice didn't sound quite so uneven, "the biggest reason I didn't go with you to New York was simple. You never asked me."

There. She'd finally said it, spoken the words out loud. In doing so, she finally faced them for the first time.

"Would you have gone?" he asked in a neutral tone.

Who knew the answer to that at this late date? The whole point was he *hadn't* asked. He hadn't even acted as though he'd given such an idea a thought. And Penny had been faced with the harsh reality of their shared life. At one time Brad Crawford had been everything in the world to her while he had considered her a friend—his buddy, a pal.

"It hardly matters at this point, does it?" she asked, staring unseeingly out the window.

"Have you ever thought about trying to make it as an actress?" he asked.

"Not for years, Brad. I'm content with my life."

"You keep saying that, but I'm not sure which one of us you're trying to convince. You were always such a natural on stage, you know. You seemed to come alive. It was a beautiful thing to see." He glanced at her, but she had her head down and he couldn't see her expression. "Don't you ever miss it?"

"Not really. I'm active with the local group...and I directed the high school play this year."

"When you could be starring on Broadway? Penny, that's a shameful waste of your talent and you know it!"

Once again she made no response.

Forcing a lighter tone, Brad asked, "What does Gregory think of your acting abilities?"

"He's never seen them," she muttered.

"But he knows about them, surely."

Penny rested her head against the window. "He knows I've had training in that area and assumes I minored in drama while I was getting my degree in education."

"Why haven't you told him? Showed him your clippings and reviews?"

She shrugged. "There's no reason to. That's just part of my past."

Brad wondered if he was too late. Was it even his place to attempt to save her? Obviously she didn't see herself as needing saving. She had chosen not only the man, but an entire way of life, and she was within days of cementing that relationship.

How could he let her do such a thing? Yet how could he, in good conscience, interfere if that was what she wanted?

He loved her. He had always loved her. He would always love her. And he wanted her to be happy. For years he had hoped that her happiness would lie with him. He'd listened to both sets of parents as they had urged him not to rush into a permanent relationship too early in their lives. They had insisted that each of them needed some space, a chance to mature separately, in order to recognize their own feelings.

So he had taken their advice. Because of it, he had lost Penny. He had wanted to be fair, and to do what was best for both of them. Instead, he had lost the only woman who had ever meant a damn to him.

But even in his worst nightmare it never occurred to him that Penny would turn into this subdued, quiet woman who was willing to accept so little in her life.

Now that Brad had brought up his move to New York, the past began to tumble into Penny's consciousness like a child's building blocks. They fell in colorful disarray around her. Mr. Akin at the post office had been right. She and Brad had been inseparable as far back as she could remember. Had anyone asked her back then, Penny would probably have explained that she and Brad would marry someday.

Strange how things had worked out.

She and Brad had never talked about their feelings for each other. There had been no reason to. They were so much a part of each other's life—until Brad announced his intention to go to New York.

Penny could still remember the day he told her. They had been home from college a week and had taken his family's boat out on the lake. The day had been warm and they had found a quiet spot to anchor and laze in the sun.

Penny had been almost asleep when Brad spoke.

"Have you decided what you want to do now that we're out of school, Runt?"

"I'm doing it," she replied in a sleepy voice.

"I mean, to earn a living?"

"I filled out an application to teach. I suppose I'll wait to hear from the school board. Why do you ask?"

He was silent so long that Penny eventually opened her eyes. He had turned so that he was facing her, and she found herself staring into his eyes. "I've decided to go to New York."

She smiled because they had talked about New York for the past year. "To become rich and famous?" she asked with a grin.

"I won't know until I try," he answered in a quiet tone.

Penny's smile slowly disappeared. "You're serious, aren't you?" she asked, and even now she could recall the sudden jolt to her system as the fear of losing him swept over her.

"Yes."

Penny never knew how she managed to get through that day. She'd fought hard to hide her reaction. Somehow it had been important for her not to let him know how devastated she felt. If he could so calmly plan his life apart from her, then she must not mean as much to him as he meant to her.

She determinedly hung on to her pride.

Penny had kept up the act of well-wishing friend until Brad left home. Only then did the true enormity of what had happened sweep over her.

Brad Crawford had blithely and without a care walked out of Penny's life. He didn't need her to make his life complete. Penny had never known such rejection, nor did she know how to deal with it.

As the months went by Penny mentally packed away all of their shared memories methodically and with grim determination. Obtaining the teaching position had been her salvation. She threw herself into the new experiences of teaching and interacting with students and co-workers. Penny learned to hide her thoughts and feelings from others, relieved to discover after a while that her highly charged emotions seemed to disappear.

When Gregory came into her life she was content. He filled a place in her daily routine. He offered companionship and conversation, all she really wanted anymore in a relationship.

Penny had overcome the pain and desolation she had felt when Brad had left. She'd forgotten, until now, what a hole he'd left in her life. Penny knew she could never allow anyone to become so important to her again.

As they continued following the country road, Penny slowly became aware of their surroundings. They had been steadily winding through the rolling hills for miles, she realized with dismay. Brad turned into the entrance of a state park and followed the road toward the bluffs where they had spent countless hours as children.

"What are we doing out here?" she demanded. "I thought we were going to get a drink?"

Brad began to laugh. "I wondered when you were going to notice."

"Brad, I don't have time to be out here. I've got to get home. I told Mother I'd be back by—" she glanced at her watch "—by now, darn you!"

"Okay, so you're late. Big deal. She knows you're with me. I thought it might be fun to come out here again. I haven't been to the park in years. I threw some snacks in a sack and brought some cold drinks. Why don't we wander around for a while, relax and enjoy the scenery? I'll take you back home whenever you say."

"Why is it I've never trusted you when you've used that tone of voice?"

"I have no idea. Everyone else always has."

"I know. But no one else knows you the way I do."

"Good point, Penny. You might want to think about just what that means to both of us. It could surprise you."

Chapter Three

Brad and Penny spent the next hour hiking along the bluffs, skipping rocks across the water and wading in the shallows—all activities they had shared during their years together.

Penny realized that, like Sonia, she really was interested in hearing how Brad had adjusted to suddenly being thrust into the limelight of the entertainment world. She plied him with countless questions—some serious, others teasing, and he patiently answered them, one by one.

When he grew tired of sitting quietly, Brad started a game of tag, and Penny seemed to forget her dignified years and chased him, convinced that he would be too out of shape to give her much trouble. She was wrong. Whatever he did in New York to keep in condition, it certainly worked.

Eventually they threw themselves on the grassy bank of the slow-moving river where they had left their food. Brad reached into the water and pulled out two soda cans dripping with water and handed her one. Penny was convinced that nothing had ever tasted so good.

"See? I told you I'd buy you a drink," he pointed out with a grin. He couldn't help but appreciate the fact that she no longer looked like the prim and proper Ms. Blackwell who was marrying the regal Mr. Duncan in a week. She'd lost the combs that had held her hair away from her face, so that the curls tumbled riotously around her cheeks and across her forehead.

Her face was flushed from running, and she was still breathing hard. The thin tank top did nothing to disguise the sauciness of her heaving breasts. Perspiration dotted her upper lip, and Brad had an almost uncontrollable urge to reach over and wipe it away with his thumb.

How could he possibly give up this woman? He had thought he would go out of his mind for the first several months he'd spent in New York. Only the remembered conversations with first her parents, then his, enabled him to recognize that before he asked her to marry him, Brad owed Penny a chance to have a life apart from him.

Their parents had known how to get him to give her time. They had pointed out that she would probably marry him out of habit, because she was used to following his lead. Did he really want a bride who accepted him for that reason? They had already known the only answer he could live with.

"What's the matter? Do I have dirt on my face?" Penny asked with a grin, looking totally relaxed and unconcerned with her appearance. She was stretched out on the grass on her side, propped up enough so that she could drink from the can without spilling it. In her shorts and skimpy top she reminded him of the young girl he'd known, free and uninhibited.

"Don't you always?" he teased. "I think you must bury your nose in the dirt every so often."

She broke off some blades of grass and tossed them at him, then laughed as they decorated his shirt. "You aren't much better, you know. Just look at your shoe."

They both gazed at his foot. His shoe and sock still dripped muddy water where he'd slipped off one of the rocks when they'd crossed the shallows. "What would your fans think of you now, Mr. Crawford?"

"I hope they would realize that I haven't enjoyed myself so much in years," he said with a smile. He gave up trying to resist temptation and reached over, running his thumb lightly across her upper lip.

Penny jerked her head, startled by his touch. His eyes were filled with golden sunshine, their toffee color warm and inviting.

"I'm not going to hurt you," he said softly.

"I didn't think you were," she admitted. "You just startled me, that's all."

Brad chose not to pursue her reactions to him. At the moment it was enough for him to see her looking so relaxed and at ease.

He rolled over onto his back and stared up at the trees above them. Sunlight dappled the ground around them, the leaves forming a canopy above. "We had some good times together, didn't we, Runt?" he asked.

She nodded.

"Do you remember the time you lost your glasses and accused me of hiding them from you?"

She laughed. "Yes."

"I almost got a beating for that. My folks believed you."

"I wonder why? You were always hiding something of mine—my baseball glove, my volleyball."

"Maybe so," he admitted, "but never your glasses. You couldn't see a thing without them."

"How well I remember."

"Contacts made a big difference for you, I know."

"You're right. A whole new world opened up. Particularly when I got the extended wear. Do you have any idea how wonderful it is to wake up at night and be able to see the clock without putting on my glasses?"

"Weren't you ashamed of accusing me of taking them and getting me in trouble?"

"Wel-l-l, maybe. But I'm sure you did a lot of things and never got caught, so it probably all evened out."

He reached over and touched her hand. "I've really missed you, Runt."

Penny looked at him a long time without speaking. "I missed you, too," she said, finally. "For the longest time I didn't think I'd ever be happy without you in my life." She began to smile. "Isn't that crazy? Now I have a whole new life separate from yours, and everything in my life is just perfect."

She looked over at him and idly noted that he had closed his eyes. His thick lashes rested on his high cheekbones. "Do you remember how we always used to argue? It drove our mothers nuts."

"Yeah, but all they had to do was find something to get our minds off whatever we were arguing about."

"Are you saying we argued out of boredom? Surely not."

Without opening his eyes he said. "You were always such a tomboy, no bigger than a minute, convinced you could do anything anyone else could do, and you usually managed to prove it no matter how hard I argued against you."

"I can remember a few times when you managed to help me in such a way that nobody else knew I hadn't done it all myself."

He smiled to himself. "That's what friends are for."

"Yes," she said with a hint of surprise. "I guess it is."

The quietness of the park settled over them, and Penny laid her head on her folded arms. She was probably going to be sore tomorrow with all of her unaccustomed exercise today. Her eyes drifted closed.

The park was so peaceful. She'd just rest her eyes for a few moments and . . .

"Penny? You'd better wake up. I'm afraid we both fell asleep."

Penny sat up with a start. The sun had almost set, and she glanced at her watch in dismay. "Oh, no! Gregory was supposed to pick me up almost half an hour ago." She came to her feet and stared up at Brad and his rueful expression.

"I'm sorry, Runt. I didn't mean this to happen," he said softly.

The sincerity in his voice couldn't be mistaken. Quickly slipping her sandals on, Penny said, "It was just as much my fault as yours." She hoped Gregory would understand. She'd never been late for a date before. He was such a stickler for promptness.

Her life seemed to be falling into a shambles since Brad had appeared, although she couldn't really hold him responsible. He just seemed to have that effect on her. Life never seemed to be as serious when he was around. And it was a lot more fun.

They were quiet in the car going back. Penny tried to prepare herself for her coming meeting with Gregory. Surely he would understand. The time had seemed to slip away. Besides, she had needed that day. It was a day apart from her life, apart from time, separate and complete. She and Brad had returned to their childhood, the innocence of youth where time was meaningless because there was so much of it.

Surely Gregory would understand. If only she could think of a more logical explanation.

But she wasn't sorry for going to the park with Brad. At least she could be honest about that. She had enjoyed every minute, even the argument in the car with Brad earlier.

There was no reason to expect Brad to approve of the man she married. She was certain that Brad would never find a woman that was good enough for him in her estimation. The thought gave her quite a pang in the region of her heart.

Penny had been careful not to ask Brad about the women he had dated, many of whom he'd been photographed with. She hadn't wanted to know about them. She knew she was being silly, but she couldn't help it. Brad was very special to her and it was time she acknowledged that to herself.

He always would be.

As soon as they pulled up in the driveway, Gregory stepped out on the front porch of the Blackwell home. Penny took a quick inventory of what she and Brad looked like and almost groaned aloud. They both had grass stains on their clothes, and his shoe looked much the worse for a dip in the river. Her hair, from the glimpse she had gotten in the side mirror, looked as if she had styled it with an eggbeater.

She felt as though they had been caught skipping school as they walked up the sidewalk toward the well-dressed man who waited for them.

"I'm glad to see you two are all right. We'd begun to worry about you," he said calmly.

Penny smiled in relief. He didn't seem at all angry but showed a perfectly natural concern. Before she could say anything, Brad said, "I really am sorry about today, Gregory. But you see, after all that physical exertion we fell asleep and weren't aware of the hours passing." His tone and smile were friendly and nonchalant.

Penny saw Gregory's body stiffen and his expression freeze. Quickly reviewing what Brad had just said, her eyes widened with horror. Of course he'd told the truth, it was just that . . .

"How interesting," Gregory said. "Perhaps you'd like to go into a little more detail. Helen said you'd gone for a drink. I never considered that to be physically taxing, myself."

"Oh, Gregory, he didn't mean that the way—" Penny began, only to have Brad interrupt her.

"Why don't you run upstairs and get cleaned up, Runt? I'll be glad to make our explanations to your fiancé. After all, he has every right to want to know how you spend your time with me."

Penny glanced uncertainly at Brad, then at Gregory. Brad still sounded casually friendly, but there was a tautness in his stance as he stood facing Gregory that contradicted his tone.

"Good idea, Penny," Gregory agreed quietly. "We're running quite late as it is."

She glanced over her shoulder at the two men as she opened the screen door. Neither one of them had moved. They seemed to be waiting for her to leave before continuing the conversation.

Penny could have cheerfully wrung Brad's neck. There was absolutely no reason for the innuendos.

What was he trying to do, give Gregory the wrong idea about their relationship?

The warm spray from the shower soothed her and Penny tried to relax. Brad had always had the ability to turn her world upside down. Why did she think anything had changed? However, she had complete faith in Gregory's ability to see through Brad's teasing and desire to cause mischief.

It would do no good for her to ask Brad to lay off. He would see that only as a challenge. So the next best thing would be to make sure she kept the two men apart. After all, it would be for only a few days, then Brad would be out of their lives once again.

When she returned downstairs Gregory was waiting alone in the living room.

She looked at him in surprise. "Where is everybody?"

"I convinced your parents to go to their dinner engagement earlier. If something had happened, I told them I'd get in touch."

Once again Penny felt guilty at her unusual and irresponsible behavior. How could she explain what she didn't understand herself?

"I really am sorry for making you wait," she said.

Gregory took her arm and escorted her outside. "Let's forget it, shall we?" he said, helping her into the car. "I managed to get our reservations changed, so there's no harm done."

Gregory was quiet on the way to the restaurant and Penny searched for something to say. Finally she asked, "Did Brad tell you we went to the park?"

He glanced at her with an enigmatic expression. "He did mention that, yes."

"It was so beautiful there. I'd forgotten how much I enjoyed being out of doors." She wondered when she had lost touch with nature. Her schedule didn't seem to include outdoor activities. Impulsively she turned to Gregory and said, "I wish you'd been with us."

Penny tried to picture Gregory hiking and wading but it was difficult. She couldn't see him laughing about his shoes getting wet or muddy. Gregory would have been out of place. She and Brad had been reliving their childhood, falling back into a familiar pattern, one in which Gregory did not fit.

"From the description that Crawford gave, I don't think I would have enjoyed the afternoon very much," Gregory said.

Even though Penny had just reached the same conclusion she was surprised to hear Gregory echo her thoughts. "Why not?"

"I generally get my exercise playing racquetball or tennis."

"Oh." Funny, they'd never discussed hobbies that much. Gregory had been so busy with his law practice since she had met him that she assumed he didn't have time for many activities. Everytime she felt that she knew him, Gregory revealed another facet of his personality. She wondered if he felt the same way about her.

Was it ever possible to find out everything about a person before you married? It wasn't that anyone deliberately omitted telling the other some things. There was just so much to learn about another person. Gregory had spent thirty-nine years doing things she knew nothing about. She'd spent twenty-five. How could you possibly catch up on everything? And how did you decide what was important to know before the wedding, rather than learning about it in the years after?

They had a quiet dinner at one of the nicer restaurants located near the interstate highway. Penny asked intelligent questions about some of Gregory's cases, drawing him out so that she could feel closer to him somehow.

One of the things that she admired most about him was his dignity in all situations. He always handled himself well. Tonight he could have justifiably shown anger and spoiled their time together. Instead, he seemed to have forgotten the less than auspicious beginning of their evening, relegating it to its rightful place of unimportance in their life.

Their life together would be one of consideration and understanding, of communication. There would be no arguments, such as she had with Brad. She and Gregory would calmly discuss then decide what needed to be faced in their shared existence. There would be no sudden bursts of emotion. Instead, they would share a sense of calmness and serenity.

After dinner Gregory suggested they move into the lounge for after-dinner drinks. A small combo played quiet music and Gregory asked her to dance. Penny willingly agreed. Gregory was an excellent dancer. Penny felt relaxed and totally at ease when they returned to their table after dancing a medley of slow numbers.

Gregory took her hand in his. He seemed to study it for some time before he looked up at her, his gray eyes serious.

"Why have you never mentioned Brad to me, Penny?"

She had been lulled into a relaxed state and his question dumped her out of the soft, fluffy cloud she'd been enjoying for the past hour or so. Penny stared at him with dismay. She had never seen quite that look on his face before. She wondered if that was the look he gave a witness just prior to cross-examination?

Not that it mattered, really. She had nothing to hide. "I don't really know, Gregory," she answered with a slight shrug. "I suppose it's because I never thought him important enough to mention."

His expression gave no indication of what he was thinking. "Not important enough, or too important to discuss?" he asked quietly.

How should she answer that? Penny had only begun to realize earlier that day that her feelings toward Brad were not as clear-cut as she had thought. "We're just friends," she offered tentatively, wondering what had prompted Gregory's line of questioning.

"I realize that. Since I've known you, I've met many of your friends, and you've talked of several others—some you knew here in Payton who later moved away, others you met at college with whom you continue to keep in touch. But you never mentioned Brad's name.''

How could she not have been aware of the omission? she wondered. She shook her head. "I really can't explain it, Gregory. Is it important?''

"Not particularly. I find it a puzzle, that's all. And I've got the sort of mind that can't leave a puzzle alone until it's solved.''

"I don't see much of a puzzle about it," she offered. "Brad's been gone for three years. He's no longer a part of my life.''

"But he was.''

"Yes. Do you have a problem with that?''

"Not necessarily. How does he feel about our getting married?''

Penny remembered Brad's earlier comments and knew she couldn't share what Brad had said with Gregory. "He wants me to be happy," she finally responded, realizing the truth of that statement.

"I'm surprised he doesn't think you'd be happier with him.''

She grinned. "Brad? You mean you think Brad wants to marry me?" She laughed. "No way. He enjoys his freedom too much.''

Gregory didn't respond. Instead, he took a sip of his drink and said, "I received a call today that means I have to go back to St. Louis. I'll be there all of next week.''

Penny gave him a stricken look. "But I thought you had arranged to be here the week before the wedding.''

"I had. I've had to rearrange my entire schedule. Unfortunately, it can't be helped. I doubt that I'll make it back much before the wedding rehearsal Friday night."

Penny felt the weight of her disappointment settle on her. Of course his law practice came first. She had always known that. At least he wasn't suggesting they postpone the wedding. After all the planning and hundreds of details, Penny shuddered to think of what it would take to change their plans now.

"I understand," she said quietly, accepting what she knew she couldn't change.

Gregory smiled. "Thank you for being so understanding. I appreciate your willingness to accommodate yourself to my schedule." He picked up his drink. "I'm glad we decided not to have the rehearsal dinner. I would have been pressed for time to have to arrange one."

"It's okay. My friends understand."

"I feel so fortunate to have found you. Nothing seems to upset you. You handle everything with such calmness."

Penny smiled. "It's taken a while for me to reach this point, let me tell you. I used to have a fiery temper."

"Well, I'm pleased that you are no longer bothered by it. The last thing I want to face at the end of one of my work days is a display of emotional fireworks." He reached over and patted her hand. "Your serenity is one of the first things that drew me to you. That, and your calm ability to handle people. Nothing ever seems to catch you off balance."

Penny thought of Brad's unexpected return and her reaction. Gregory had accurately described the person she thought she was, except when Brad was around. He seemed to trigger emotional depths in her that almost frightened her. She didn't like the emotional, out-of-control-person Brad seemed to bring forth in her with no apparent effort.

What a lucky escape she'd had, discovering what an adverse effect Brad had on her.

Later Gregory drove her home, walked her to the door and refused to come inside with her.

"It's late, love, and I have a full day's work on my desk tomorrow before I can even leave for St. Louis."

"Will I see you before you go?"

"I really don't think so, although there's nothing I'd like more than to spend tomorrow with you. However, I don't see how I can possibly get away, not when I'm going to be gone for a week on our honeymoon."

He leaned down and kissed her. Stepping back, he smiled and said, "If I don't stop that, I'll never get away from you tonight. Sleep well, my love." Gregory waited until she went inside and locked the door, then walked to his car. He glanced at the house next door.

Penny had brushed his questions aside regarding Brad Crawford. But there was something there and Gregory knew it. He'd sensed Brad's carefully concealed emotions the night before and earlier this evening. His light, casual air had been very well done.

Gregory hadn't been misled. He'd made a career studying human behavior. The man was in love with Penny.

The question was, how did Penny feel about Brad? And how would her feelings for Brad affect her marriage to Gregory?

Gregory drove back to town in deep thought.

Chapter Four

Penny slept restlessly that night. Her dreams were all mixed up. There seemed to be two men wandering through them—one calm and filled with authority, the other laughing and teasing her.

Scraps of conversation danced in her head. She heard Brad asking, "Come to New York with me...come with me...with me...me..."

Gregory appeared. He paced before her as she sat at the witness stand. He kept demanding, over and over, "What is your relationship to this man?" He would point to a cage in the corner of the room. When Penny looked inside the cage Brad sat there—a ten-year-old Brad with his baseball cap and ragged sneakers on.

No matter what she tried to say, Gregory continued to ask, "What is your relationship to this man?"

"Penny, you're going to be late for church if you don't get up soon, dear," Helen called through her closed door.

Penny groaned and pulled her pillow over her head, trying to drown out her mother's voice and the bright sunlight that streamed through her window.

What had happened to the night's rest she'd come to take for granted over the years? Penny felt as though she'd been up all night in some philosophical debate. Bits of her dreams came back to her, but they didn't make sense. Why would she have dreamed of a young Brad in a cage?

She forced herself up, trying to get her eyelids to stay open. Having Brad home was having a definite effect on her. She wished she could understand it. For the past three years she had built a life for herself, on her own, without Brad's influence.

Within a day of his return, she'd reverted to allowing him to influence her. Take yesterday, for example. They'd played in the park like a couple of kids. *You enjoyed it, though, didn't you,* the little voice inside of her said.

Of course I enjoyed it.

Then what are you complaining about?

She really wasn't sure. There seemed something rather childish about enjoying herself, but she couldn't quite decide what it was.

Penny wandered into her bathroom and turned on the shower. Her mother had been right. If she didn't hurry, she'd be late for church.

By the time she was dressed and grabbed some toast and coffee, Penny was late for the church service. She waited outside the sanctuary doors until after the opening prayer, then slipped into the pew where her family generally sat.

While she hastily thumbed through the hymnal for the first selection she glanced around her. Gregory had become a member of the church and, unless he was out of town, he usually attended Sunday services, but she didn't see him this morning.

The congregation was well into the second verse of the hymn when someone paused by the pew. Penny became aware that someone else was later than she was. She looked up, half expecting Gregory. Instead, Brad edged into the pew beside her and took one side of her hymnbook in a silent request to share.

He looked rested and well-groomed and when she met his eyes he gave her a smile that would have warmed the heart of the coldest critic.

Penny felt her own heart sink. She didn't want to see Brad Crawford. Not today. Not until she was able to get her life back into some sort of order. Whether she liked it or not, Brad was a definite distraction to her.

What would Gregory think if he saw them standing there together, after his questions last night? Why hadn't she ever mentioned Brad to Gregory before?

Could it be she was ashamed of their relationship? How absurd. That would be the same as saying she was ashamed of herself. Brad was so much a part of her he seemed to be an extension of herself. Funny she'd never really thought about that before this weekend.

She'd been so hurt when he went to New York. But it had been good for her. She'd gotten in touch with herself and her own views and goals. If Brad hadn't gone away she probably would have drifted into marriage with him, just because he was so familiar.

What would be wrong with that? that tiny voice asked.

I'm marrying Gregory! He's more my type, she responded sternly. *I don't want to hear any more of your irresponsible remarks.*

The pew where they stood was full. When the hymn was concluded and everyone sat down, Brad was pressed against her side, from shoulder to thigh. She tried to shift but it didn't seem to help. Finally, he placed his arm on the back of the pew, giving them a little extra space, but creating a visual intimacy between them that Penny could have easily done without.

Whenever she glanced at him, Brad responded with a look of smiling inquiry.

He certainly seemed pleased with himself this morning, she thought waspishly. Obviously nothing had disturbed *his* sleep last night.

Penny realized later that she hadn't heard a word the pastor had said during his sermon. It was only when he mentioned the announcements in the bulletin and she heard her name that Penny became aware that she'd missed most of the service.

"You will note that this coming Saturday Gregory Duncan and Penny Blackwell will be joined in Holy Matrimony before this altar," Reverend Wilder said with a smile. "The Blackwells have extended an invitation to each and every one of you to join them in celebrating their daughter's wedding and hope to see you there."

Penny felt as though a spotlight had fallen on her and Brad as they sat there so closely. She forced herself to keep her eyes trained on Reverend Wilder, whose friendly smile served as a beacon of sanity in her sea of confusion. *This, too, shall pass.* The thought seemed to flow around her and she gained some comfort from it.

As soon as the final song was sung she was ready to bolt from the church and search for solitude.

Instead, it seemed as though everyone who attended church that morning wanted to stop and speak to her... and to Brad, who continued to stand beside her in the crowd.

"My, if it doesn't look natural to see the two of you together again," one woman said with a smile after she had greeted them.

"It's good to see you, Mrs. Fielding," Brad replied easily. Her husband owned the local hardware store and had been Brad's coach during his years of Little League.

"I don't suppose you came back in time to stop the wedding now, did you, young man?" she said archly and Penny suddenly prayed for a trap door that would allow her to drop out of sight.

Brad just laughed.

Mrs. Cantrell joined them. "Where is your young man this morning, Penny? When I first saw you standing there this morning, I thought Brad was your Mr. Duncan."

"I'm not sure where Gregory is, Mrs. Cantrell. How's Mr. Cantrell's leg?"

"Oh, it's healing right nicely. He was just lucky he didn't lose it, being so careless around the farm machinery." Not to be led astray from her subject, she went on. "Guess Mr. Duncan can find better things to do with his time than to go to church on Sunday. Those big city people don't seem to consider it as important as some of us," she said with a sniff.

"Oh, I'm sure it's nothing like that, Mrs. Cantrell. But since we're going to be away for a week, Gregory's been putting in long hours trying to clear his calendar."

"Well, it's sure good to see you here, Brad," Mrs. Cantrell said without commenting on Penny's explanation. "Wish you were going to be back home all the time."

Brad grinned. "Well, if there's some way I could convince the production crew to film *Hope for Tomorrow* here in Payton, I'd move back in a flash."

Everyone laughed, except Penny, who had a sudden vision of what life would be like if Brad lived there full time. Her beautifully planned future would probably become a shambles! She edged her way around the group that had gathered just outside the church doors. She'd almost made it to her car when Brad caught up with her.

"Mind if I get a ride home with you?"

"What's wrong with your car?"

"As you know, I've been using Mom's car. It wouldn't start this morning, so I got a ride in with Mom and Dad. They were on their way to visit friends for the day."

"I'm surprised you didn't go with them," Penny said, giving in to the inevitable and motioning for him to get in.

"I thought about it, but decided I'd rather spend the day with you."

"Why?" she asked baldly.

He looked at her in surprise, noticing for the first time the dark shadows under her eyes. "Why?" he repeated. "Do I have to have a reason to want to spend the day with you?"

She shrugged. "What if I've already made plans?"

"Have you?"

Good question. Gregory hadn't called before she left, but he'd made it clear today would be extremely busy for him. She'd be lucky to receive a phone call before he left for St. Louis.

She glanced over at Brad. "Not really," she admitted.

"Why don't we take the boat out on the lake?" he suggested. "It looks like a perfect day for it."

Penny thought about his suggestion for a moment. She enjoyed nothing more than being out on the water. The lake had been formed by a dam built over the river. When they were younger she and Brad had spent many a day following the river and exploring some of the coves that had formed when the water backed up.

The thought of a peaceful cove somewhere seemed to be an excellent idea. "All right," she agreed.

"Do you suppose you could find your way around your mom's kitchen enough to make us something to take along to eat?" Brad asked with a grin.

She refused to rise to the bait. "I'm sure I can. It would probably astound you how well I manage on my own these days."

He watched her in silence as they turned down the road that led to their homes. "Is something wrong, Penny?"

Funny he should ask. "What could possibly be wrong, Brad? I'm getting married in six days. Everything is perfect." She refused to look at him.

"You look tired."

"I've been keeping a busy schedule. School was just out and I've had a lot to do, getting ready for the wedding."

Brad said nothing more and Penny found some comfort in the ensuing silence.

Hours later, Penny knew she'd been right to accept Brad's invitation. This was just what she needed. Her sleek, one-piece suit was great to swim in. They had found a cove where they could swim without being afraid of being run over by a boat hauling water-skiers.

Brad and Penny had spent as much time in the water as they could all the years they'd lived at the lake. Consequently they were very much at home in it. They were like a pair of porpoises playing and they quickly returned to the pattern of their childhood. Once again, Penny forgot about Gregory and his promise to call her.

By the time they decided to eat, both of them were laughing and winded.

Penny had cheated. She had raided the refrigerator, knowing her mother wouldn't care. There had been leftover chicken, some ham, potato salad and fresh vegetables, all peeled and sliced. And for dessert, she had cut giant slices of her mother's cherry-chocolate cake.

By the time they finished eating, they felt too lazy to move.

"When do you have to get back?" Brad asked, squinting up at the sun as though trying to decide the time.

"No particular time, I suppose."

"Is Gregory coming over?"

Gregory. She hadn't given him a thought for several hours. A surge of guilt flooded through her. No doubt he'd spent the day working while she was out playing like some carefree teenager.

Brad seemed to have that effect on her. She didn't understand it. When she was with Gregory, she behaved as a mature adult would. Somehow Brad brought out the child in her.

"He didn't say," she finally said, in response to Brad's question.

"I suppose he's really busy."

"Yes."

"He appears to be very successful."

"Yes."

"Must put in some long hours."

"He has, ever since I've known him."

"Doesn't have much time to relax and enjoy himself, then," Brad offered.

Penny glanced over at him thoughtfully. "I think he enjoys himself. His practice is something he enjoys. Not only is it his vocation, it's his avocation as well."

"Do you think you're going to be happy with that sort of life, Penny?" Brad asked. His serious expression let her know he was really concerned.

She leaned back on the cushioned seat. "I won't mind it. I'm busy, too, not only with teaching but with the theater group. We each have our own lives, but we enjoy each other's company as well."

"It seems such a tepid existence for you, of all people."

She sat up and looked at him with a hint of indignation. "What do you mean me, 'of all people'?"

"Oh, you know, Runt. You're so full of life and vitality, your energy never seems to run down. I can't see all of that passion bottled into such a tame existence."

She laughed. "You're crazy. I'm not some wild, passionate creature who craves excitement."

"Maybe not. But you could be. The only time you let it loose is on stage. You've never allowed it to show, except when you lose your temper."

"Which I never do, except when you're around."

"Why do you suppose that is?"

"Besides the fact that you can be extremely aggravating at times and more than a little irritating at other times?" She widened her eyes in an innocent stare. "Why, I have no idea, Mr. Crawford. None at all."

He leaned back so that he was stretched full length across the rear of the boat. "I came home to break up your engagement," he said in a matter-of-fact tone.

His quiet statement caused her to come out of her seat. "You did what?"

"You heard me."

"How dare you even consider it!"

"I know. I finally came to the same conclusion."

She stared at him in disbelief. "But why would you even want to?"

He shrugged. "It doesn't really matter now. Since I've met him, and talked with you, I realize that if he's what you want I have no right to cause problems for you."

The idea that he had even thought of doing such a thing infuriated her. "Just who in the hell do you think you are—God?"

"No. But I am your friend. I care what happens to you. I didn't want you to make a mistake."

"And you think you know better than I do what's best for me?" she demanded to know.

"Obviously not, or I would have gone through with it."

"Fat chance, you egotistical, arrogant boob. I believe your new status and identity have gone to your head!"

"Aw, come on, Runt, you know better than that."

"And stop calling me that revolting name."

"You never used to mind it."

"Well, I certainly do now. It was all right when I was a child. It sounds perfectly ridiculous now."

Penny couldn't remember the last time she had felt such anger. Whenever it was, she was certain that it had been directed toward Brad then, as well. He was the most impossible, infuriating—she couldn't find enough names to call him.

"I want to go home," she said in carefully level tones. *Before I attempt bodily harm on you,* she added silently. To think that she had considered him a friend. But no friend would even consider doing to her what he had admitted planning.

Brad sat up. "Fine with me."

She turned the blower switch on, giving time for the fumes to clear before starting the boat. Without another word, they began to pack up the remains of their lunch. Then Penny, being the closest, started the boat and began to leave the cove.

As soon as they cleared the cove she moved the throttle to pick up speed. Out of the corner of her eye she caught a movement and glanced around in time to see another boat shooting around the point, coming directly at her. Pure reflex saved them from a nasty collision.

Penny yelled and jerked the steering wheel hard, cutting their speed at the same time. The combination of suddenly turning and losing speed caused quite a reaction on board and Penny heard a commotion of bumps and Brad's yell behind her.

The other boat went by. It was filled with a bunch of teenagers who were laughing and waving at her.

"Stupid jerks!" she yelled. "Don't you have any better sense? If you don't know water safety you should stay off the lake!" She doubted that they heard her words, but she felt better. Turning around she began to say, "I'm sorry, Brad, I hope you didn't—"

He was crumpled on the deck, the ice chest lying on top of him.

"Brad!" Penny scrambled over a loose oar, life jackets and other paraphernalia that had spilled out during the near-collision. She knelt by his side. Shoving the cooler aside she reached for him. His color seemed to be gone and he wasn't moving. "Brad?" There was a gash at his temple, and blood seemed to be everywhere. "Oh, God! Brad!"

He didn't respond.

Frantic, Penny looked around. They had come a few miles from home. There was nothing on shore that indicated people might be close by. Even in her panic she knew she had to get help. The closest she could think of was home.

Penny grabbed a towel and began to clean the blood from his face. She held pressure there until the flow eased up. Then she gently checked to see if she could find any other injuries.

He was out cold and she didn't know how badly he'd been hit. There was nothing more she could do now. She had to get him to the hospital as quickly as possible.

Penny didn't even realize she was crying until she had to keep blinking to see where she was going on the way home.

Brad was hurt and it was her fault. She'd been so mad at him. She'd even thought about doing him bodily harm! And look what had happened. "I didn't mean it, God! You know I didn't mean it. Don't let it be serious. Please. Please let him be all right."

She set new speed records getting home. As soon as she could tie up the boat at her dock she ran up the path. "Mom! Dad! Call the ambulance, Brad's been hurt!"

Penny burst into the house, gasping for breath. Gregory met her by the time she reached the kitchen, her parents right behind him. She absently noticed his casual dress but she had no time to question him.

"What's the matter!" he demanded.

"It's Brad! He fell. Hit his head. He's bleeding and I don't know how badly he's hurt."

He grabbed her by the shoulders. "All right, now. Calm down. You call an ambulance and we'll go check on him."

Quickly she nodded, reaching for the wall phone and glancing at the emergency number posted nearby.

Later, Penny couldn't seem to remember all of the events. She knew Gregory and her dad had gone down to the landing and had brought Brad up to the house. He was still unconscious.

She'd called his parents and they were all there when the ambulance arrived. Without thinking about it, Penny crawled into the ambulance with him, holding his hand and whispering to him. "I'm sorry, Brad. I never meant to hurt you. You know that. It was just a crazy accident. Please get better, Brad. Please don't be hurt bad."

The attendant handed her a tissue and she realized that tears still streamed down her face.

The doctor was waiting for them when they arrived and it was only when they'd taken him into the examining room that Penny realized she was standing barefoot in her bathing suit.

Both sets of parents and Gregory arrived within minutes. Her mother, bless her heart, had grabbed some clean, dry clothes for her and Penny excused herself and went into the ladies' restroom to change.

As soon as she came out she asked, "Have you heard anything?"

They all shook their heads. Gregory led her to a couch that looked as though it had been brought off the ark and sat down beside her. "Can you tell us what happened?"

As coherently as possible, she explained the sequence of events. When she was finished, Gregory asked, "Could you identify the other boat or any of the people in it?"

"I doubt it. It all happened so fast. They were just a bunch of kids out having a good time and not paying attention."

"Without your quick responses, it could have been much worse, you know. They need to be found and reprimanded."

Her eyes filled once again. "It was so awful, Gregory," she said in a choked voice. "We'd been fighting and I was so blasted mad at him, but I didn't want him to get hurt." She lay her head on his shoulder and cried, her sobs shaking her body.

"I know. He's very special to you. I'm beginning to understand that."

He held her until eventually the emotional shock began to abate and she had managed to gain some measure of control.

The doctor on call appeared in the doorway of the waiting room. He was new to the area and none of them knew him.

He smiled at the three couples waiting and said, "This young man was very lucky. He did receive a concussion, but it could have been much worse. Blows to the temple are very tricky things."

Brad's mother asked, "But he's going to be all right. You're sure?"

"Oh, yes. He came to for a few minutes. He's still groggy and we gave him something to ease the pain." He paused and glanced at the three women. "Which one of you is Penny?"

Penny came to her feet. The doctor's smile widened. "You might want to go in and see him for a few minutes. He's disoriented and seems to think something happened to you. He's been calling your name and fighting me, saying he had to find you."

Without a thought Penny joined the doctor in the doorway. "Where is he?"

He turned and started down the hallway. "We put him in this room," he said, opening the door and holding it for her.

Penny tiptoed into the room. The shades were drawn and it was dim. The doctor snapped on a nightlight and she could see Brad lying there, his head swathed in white bandages. His eyes were closed and he looked so pale. Penny bit her lip to keep from crying out.

She glanced around and discovered the doctor had left the room. Hesitantly she approached the bed. Brad was in a hospital gown and the sheet was folded neatly over his chest. His hands rested on either side of him. She took his hand and slowly lifted it to her mouth, brushing her lips across his knuckles.

Brad's lashes fluttered, then he slowly opened his eyes. "Penny?" His lips moved but there was very little sound.

"I'm here, Brad."

"You okay?" he managed to say. He was having trouble moving his mouth.

"I'm fine. It's you we've been worried about."

"Wha' happened?"

"A boat almost rammed us. I dodged to miss them and threw you halfway across our boat." Tears began to stream down her face once more. "Oh, Brad. I'm so sorry."

"Wasn't your fault," he said drowsily.

"I'm sorry I got so mad at you. I was afraid you'd been killed and I would never be able to tell you how sorry I am."

"I'm...too hard-headed...to be hurt...by a blow...to my head," he said haltingly, trying to smile. She could see the pain in his eyes and she ached with shared pain. "Besides, you had a right...to get angry at me. Trying to break...engagement...was... childish thing to do."

She smiled. "I'm afraid I have to agree with you there, my friend."

"I'm sorry...forgive me?"

She stroked his cheek with her free hand. "You know me, Brad, I can never stay mad at you for long. I never could."

"Good thing," he replied, his voice slurred. "Or you'd...be angry...all...time."

"I'm sure the doctor wants you to rest," she said. "Your folks are waiting outside. I know they want to see you."

He smiled, a slow, sleepy smile that seemed to increase the ache in her heart.

She leaned over and kissed him. "I'll see you tomorrow, Brad." She laid his hand on his chest, but she didn't let go immediately.

He squeezed her hand but didn't say anything. She

patted the hand she still held and slowly released him, suddenly feeling awkward.

Then Penny turned around and left the room.

Chapter Five

Gregory was quiet on the way home and Penny felt too drained to try to make conversation. He followed her into the house and she went to the kitchen to make coffee, motioning him into the living room.

Her parents had stayed at the hospital with the Crawfords. No one had expressed an opinion as to when they'd return.

When she brought the coffee into the living room Penny suddenly realized she had never asked Gregory why he'd been there that afternoon.

"I'm so glad you came today," she said, handing him his cup and settling beside him on the couch. "I'm just sorry I wasn't here. I thought you said you were going to spend the day working."

He looked at her and smiled, a wry smile that she found endearing. "Actually, I had no intention of leaving the office until I had made a dent in the pile of files and papers on my desk." Gregory settled back on the sofa with a sigh. "After a few hours I noticed there was no appreciable difference in the amount of work in front of me." He took a sip of coffee. "I kept thinking of you and how much I wanted to be with you."

Gregory peered into his cup as though looking for an answer to a thorny question. "As a matter of fact, I decided to forget about the work for a while and come get you. I thought we could spend some time together out on the lake."

His eyes met hers. "When I got here your parents mentioned that you and Brad had gone out a few hours earlier."

Penny touched his cheek lightly with her hand. "I wish I'd known. I could have waited."

"Spending the day with you and Brad wasn't what I had in mind."

"What I meant was that if I'd known, I would have waited and gone out with you. Brad would have found someone else to spend the day with."

Gregory studied her face, enjoying the candid expression in her blue eyes, the way her flyaway curls clustered on her forehead. Most of all he enjoyed the unconscious innocence she projected, not so much a sexual innocence, although he was willing to bet that was the case. But Penny had a wholesomeness, such a trusting nature that he sometimes felt he was hundreds of years older than she. The ugliness of the world seemed to have passed her by, as though, like a princess in a fairy tale, she had been locked away and protected from some of the harsher realities of life.

"You mentioned earlier that you and Brad had been arguing," he said with a slight smile.

Penny felt her face flush. "Yes."

"About what?"

She stared at him in dismay. She had no idea what Gregory thought of Brad. He was an expert at keeping his thoughts and opinions to himself. For some reason she didn't want him to know about Brad's intention to break them up. The point was, he hadn't and he was sorry. There was no need to share the details with Gregory.

"I can't even remember," she said, not meeting his eyes. "Brad and I seem to argue every time we're around each other."

"I still find that surprising in you."

"I know. Some people have that effect on others."

He nodded thoughtfully. "Yes, that's true. Sparks fly."

She laughed. "They definitely fly whenever Brad and I get together." She hugged Gregory. "I'm so glad you and I don't react that way to each other. I much prefer our comfortable relationship." When he didn't reply she went on to say, "I never got around to thanking you for your help today. I don't know what I would have done without you."

He held her hard against his chest, unable to resist her lips so close to his. Gregory kissed her, feeling her warmth pressed against him.

When he finally released her he smiled at the picture she made—her cheeks flushed, her eyes sparkling, her mouth slightly swollen. "I was glad to help, but you would have done just fine without me. You handled yourself extremely well in the emergency, never losing your head."

"Oh, no. I almost drowned you in my tears at the hospital."

"Yes, after the crisis was over. But when you needed to be strong you managed to give Brad first aid, then got him home. I was very proud of you today. I want you to know that."

"Oh, Gregory. Your ability to understand me is one of the things I love about you," she said, her arms still around him.

He was quiet for a few moments, then said, "It's interesting, isn't it, the many different ways we can love. Some people seem to have a larger capacity for love than others. You seem to have grown up giving your love to people—your parents, Brad, his parents; later the people who live in Payton. Now me."

She smiled at him.

"I always had trouble understanding that emotion they called love. I've seen some of the tragedies that have occurred in the name of love, witnessed selfishness and possessiveness that have been given the label of love, but until I met you, I never truly experienced what it all meant—the generosity of love for its own sake, and what a difference it could make in life." He looked down at her, trying to memorize the beauty that was in her. "Thank you for showing me how unselfish love can be, how generous."

"It was my pleasure," she said with a mischievous grin. "You've shown me a great deal, too, you know."

"Have I? In what way?"

"You didn't treat me like some fragile doll sitting on a shelf. You've always treated me as an equal, with respect and admiration."

"Hasn't everyone?"

"It's hard to explain. But living in the same small town all my life has meant that everyone has preconceived ideas about me. Until you came along, nobody would even ask me out for a date!"

"Why do you suppose they didn't?"

She grinned. "Because all the eligible men already knew me too well, I guess."

"It couldn't have anything to do with Brad, could it?"

She frowned. "What does Brad have to do with my not being asked on a date?"

"Perhaps everyone thought you two were a pair," he suggested.

Penny rolled her eyes. "That's quite possible. I know everybody acted surprised when you and I announced our engagement. I just assumed they thought you'd been tricked into proposing to me."

Gregory threw his head back and laughed and she began to laugh with him. "Oh, Penny, what an innocent you are!" He studied her for a moment, the light of laughter gradually disappearing out of his eyes. "Then you admit that people saw you and Brad as a couple."

She shrugged. "I can't very well deny it. Since he's been home everyone I've seen has made some comment. But that's their problem. It doesn't really concern you and me. Once we're married, they'll get those silly ideas out of their heads."

"So you don't really wish that it were Brad you were marrying instead of me?"

"Brad and I don't have that sort of a relationship. We never did. You are the man I'm going to marry." She sounded very final.

Gregory smiled. "I'm glad to hear it." He carefully unwrapped her arms from around his neck. "However, at the moment I think I'd better let you get some rest. I've still got to pack and get ready to return to St. Louis."

Penny hated to see him leave. She enjoyed his companionship so much. She felt safe and secure whenever he was around. In particular, she needed his presence this final week before she married him, especially now that Brad was here. She couldn't explain it. She just knew it was true. But she knew she mustn't be selfish, so she walked him to the door in silence.

He paused at the door and looked down at her. "I'm going to be extremely busy, so don't worry if you don't hear from me. I'll be back in time for the rehearsal Friday night. You can count on it."

She nodded. "I'll just think about this time next week when we'll be on our honeymoon," she said with a grin. "That should help fill the next few days."

"I'm sure you'll want to spend some time with Brad while he's recuperating." Gregory waited for a denial, for some sign that, despite everything he had seen and heard, Penny wasn't as attached to Brad as Gregory was finally coming to accept.

"Yes, that's true," she said, unaware of what he was thinking. "You know his television character is supposed to be in a coma. He almost had a chance to find out what that was like firsthand." She shook her head. "I bet he's already regretting having come home for the wedding."

"Then again, it might have been a very crucial decision for his future. Who knows?" Gregory said, leaning over and kissing her softly on the mouth. "I suppose only time will tell."

I wonder what he meant by that? Penny asked herself when she went upstairs and began to prepare for bed. Gregory could certainly be enigmatic at times. No doubt that trait was one of the reasons he was such a brilliant attorney.

"Oh, how sweet," Brad cooed in a cloying falsetto voice, clasping his hands under his chin and giving her an idiotic smile. "You brought me some candy," he said as she walked into his hospital room the next morning carrying a gaily wrapped package.

Penny was relieved to see him looking so much better. His color had improved considerably since the day before. Today he looked almost rakish with his head bandaged, but there were still deep bruises under his eyes.

"What I have is much better for you than candy," she informed him, walking over to the bed and handing him the package. "I've brought you a coloring book and some crayons." It was worth the search she'd gone to that morning to see the expression on his face.

Without missing a beat he said, "Fantastic, what kind?"

"Only the best for you, my friend—a book immortalizing the characters from *Star Wars*."

Brad started to chuckle, then gently touched his head. "Please don't make me laugh. My head feels like it's going to topple off my shoulders when I so much as move it. Laughter would destroy me."

She leaned over and kissed him on the cheek. "Poor baby. And here I thought you'd be so pleased."

"I am. I am. You're the only one who knows about my secret passion for the *Star Wars* trilogy."

"Oh, I don't think you managed to keep your deep, dark secret from your mom. Remember, she was the one who attempted to keep order in your room for years."

He smiled. "Yes, but I've learned that I can trust the two women in my life to keep my deeply-guarded secret."

"So how are you feeling?"

"Like I've spent a week wrapped around several bottles of booze and just surfaced."

"That bad, huh?"

"I knew there was a reason I never drank much. Can you imagine someone paying to feel this bad?"

"Who are you kidding? You never wanted to lose your wholesome kid image and you know it."

"Wholesome? Me? Don't let my producer hear you say that. He's convinced I look like the sort who'd start seducing maidens before breakfast and continue throughout the day without pause."

She grinned. "Are you sure that's the appeal? I always thought you looked like the sort women dreamed of being seduced by."

He eyed her speculatively. "Oh, yeah? Tell me more."

"Nothing doing. You're too vain as it is."

Brad patted the side of his bed and she perched on it. "I don't think I remembered to thank you for your help yesterday," he said.

"My help! That blow to the head must have really befuddled you, my friend. I'm afraid I was the one who caused it."

"That's not the way Dad explained it. You probably saved us both from a serious, perhaps even fatal, collision."

Penny couldn't think of anything to say. She glanced around the room, then back at him. "Has the doctor said when you're going to be able to get out of here?"

"Hopefully tomorrow. He said I would have to take it easy for a few days, but since that was the way I'd intended to spend the week anyway, I'm not going to have much trouble following the doctor's orders."

"Are you sorry you came back?" she asked quietly.

He waited until her eyes met his. They stared at each other for an indeterminable length of time. "No, I'm not sorry. My only regret is that I didn't come back sooner."

"Why do you say that?"

"It doesn't matter. Now you're deliriously in love with your handsome lawyer and soon you'll be a blushing bride and will live happily ever after." He took her hand and held it between both of his. "You know, Penny, that's all I ever wanted, for you to be happy. I've enjoyed our time together this week—the visit to the park, the fun we had yesterday."

"Some fun."

"It was, most of it. Sharing those things with you, one last time, helped me to say goodbye to our shared past. I needed the transition time, a chance to be with you before you become the oh, so proper wife of the esteemed and honorable Gregory Duncan."

"Now you're making fun of us."

"Not at all. I'm trying like hell not to envy what the two of you have."

"You'll find it for yourself, someday."

He nodded. "Of course I will."

She made a face. "And I'll hate her on sight," she admitted with a slight smile.

His eyebrows arched slightly. "Without even knowing her?"

"Without a doubt. You always had such lousy taste in women, you know."

"Oh, really?" he said in a dangerous tone.

"Yes, really! Have you forgotten dating Diana during our second year at college?"

"How could I ever forget the lovely Diana? She was a knockout."

"True. And she was also sleeping with every guy on the campus."

"Yeah, well, no man's education is quite complete without a Diana in his life," he said with a grin.

"What about Beth?"

"What was wrong with Beth?" he asked with surprise. "I thought you liked her."

"Liked her? I felt sorry for her. How she ever managed to get out of grade school, much less find her way into college, always remained a mystery to me."

"So she wasn't the brightest person we've ever known. She was very sweet."

"Yes. And she adored you."

"Can't fault her taste."

"Only her intelligence."

They paused and grinned at each other.

Brad squeezed the hand he still held. "God, I've missed you. Nobody has ever given me such a bad time, or led me in such intricate circles as you."

"Moi?" she asked in mock surprise. "Surely not."

"Why didn't you ever come to New York to see me, like I wrote and asked you to?"

Penny gazed out the window, thinking back over the years. "Because I was still too angry with you."

"Angry! What had I done?"

"You left me here and went off to continue playing at life."

"Is that what it seemed to you?"

She nodded. "I guess I had always assumed you'd come back to Payton and go to work with your dad. It never occurred to me that your talk of New York was anything but the usual chatter we all had. About the time when we'd be discovered and cast in a starring role. Or being understudy one night, stopping the show as the lead the next."

"You could still do that, you know."

"Not me. I can't see Gregory content to have a wife living half a continent away."

"There is that."

Penny slipped from the bed and brushed the wrinkles from her skirt. "I don't want to keep you from your coloring, my dear. Maybe the nurse will help you if you get too tired to finish by yourself."

Brad didn't smile but continued to look at her. His hand still grasped hers and he slowly loosened his hold. "I love you, Penny," he said, his voice so low she almost didn't hear him. "Thank you for being a part of my life."

In all the years she had known him, he had never said those words to her before. Hearing them now did something strange to her. She wanted to laugh. She wanted to cry. She wanted to throw her arms around his neck. She wanted to go running down the hall.

"I love you, too, Brad," she finally replied.

"Now's a hell of a time to let me in on that little secret," he pointed out rather grimly.

"You haven't exactly been forthcoming yourself, you know."

"I know. Words of love are too special to use lightly. But then, you're a very special person in my life. You always will be."

Penny couldn't control the tears that suddenly flooded her eyes. "You are, too."

"Remember, if you ever need me, for anything, I'll always be there for you. That's what friends are for."

She couldn't say a word. Not one. For if she did, she would end up making a complete fool of herself. So she squeezed his hand, then turned away and walked out of the room.

When Gregory called her that night she was able to report that Brad was rapidly improving and due to come home the next day.

"That's good news, I'm sure."

"Yes," she said, a little abstracted. Penny had wandered around the house all day, like a lost soul trying to find its home. "How are things going for you?" she asked, determined to concentrate on Gregory.

He filled her in on some of the complications he'd run into and she found her thoughts wandering once again. She loved Gregory; there was no way to deny what she felt for him. But it was so different from the way she felt for Brad.

Would she ever be able to forget how she felt for those few moments when she thought Brad was dead? Penny never wanted to suffer through anything so traumatic again. She couldn't begin to picture what life would be like for her if she didn't know that Brad Crawford was somewhere in the world.

"Penny?"

"Oh, I'm sorry, Gregory, I was distracted for a moment."

There was a silence for a moment before Gregory responded. "I'm not surprised," he finally said. "You've had so much on your mind, lately."

"No more than you, I'm sure."

"Yes, well, different things affect us different ways. I've got to let you go for now. I'll see you Friday night."

"Fine. Take care now."

"You, too."

Penny hung up the phone, feeling oddly restless and discontent.

For a moment she wished she could lie down and go to sleep and wake up Saturday morning in time for her wedding. The prewedding jitters were getting completely out of hand.

Brad had been home for three days when his mother called him to the phone. He assumed it was Penny checking to see how he was feeling, although she generally came over. In fact, she had promised him a game of chess sometime that day before she had to go to the church for the wedding rehearsal.

"Hello?"

"Good morning, Brad. This is Gregory Duncan. How are you feeling these days?"

To say Brad was surprised to hear from Penny's fiancé would be a definite understatement. He had assumed that Penny was reporting his progress to Gregory whenever they spoke to each other. For some reason Brad didn't feel as though he had made Gregory's best friends' list.

"I'm feeling much better, thank you."

"I was wondering if you'd feel up to meeting me somewhere. There's something I would like to discuss with you."

"Today?"

"Yes, if at all possible. Penny may have told you I've been in St. Louis all week. I just got in."

"I see," Brad said, automatically. Actually, he didn't see at all. Why was Gregory calling him? More important, why would he want to meet with him?

"Brad? Are you there?"

"Oh, sorry. I was thinking. Yes, I suppose I could meet you at your office, if that would be convenient."

"Fine. I'll see you whenever you can get here."

Brad hung up the phone, still puzzled. Maybe Penny had told Gregory about their conversation at the hospital. Was Gregory going to tell him to keep away from his wife? That was a little dramatic, but then trial attorneys had been known to use a little drama to get a point across.

Brad absently touched his head, where a small bandage covered the blow he'd received.

Perhaps the blow to his head had caused him to feel all of this confusion. Maybe he was Drew Derek, recovering from his stay at the hospital. This visit home certainly had all the elements that could be found in a soap opera.

He could almost hear the strains of music in the background while the announcer intoned—"Tune in tomorrow to find out . . . What does Gregory want to say to Brad? Does Gregory know that Brad is in love with his fiancé and had hoped to break up their engagement? Will Gregory denounce Brad to Penny? Will Brad be barred from the church for fear he might try to stop the proceedings? Stay tuned . . ."

Brad shook his head. Obviously his vacation had been long overdue. He must be cracking up.

Brad had never seen the building where Gregory Duncan had his law practice. He was impressed. The office itself was even more impressive. A middle-aged woman sat at a secretarial desk in the reception area.

"May I help you?" she asked pleasantly.

"My name is Brad Crawford. I—"

"Oh, yes, Mr. Crawford. Mr. Duncan asked that you be shown in immediately." She came around her desk and led him down a hallway lined with law books. Tapping on the door at the end, she announced, "Mr. Crawford is here," and stepped back, allowing Brad to enter.

The office was a corner one, so two walls were almost entirely made up of glass. Since the building was located on the edge of town, the view from the windows was of meadows, rolling hills and a distant glimpse of the river.

"I'm impressed," Brad said quietly, standing in the doorway.

Gregory had stood when he walked in. Now he walked around his massive desk toward Brad. The room seemed large enough to hold a basketball court. All the furniture, furnishings and the well-dressed man coming toward him spoke of dignity and wealth. How could Brad have been so stupid as to suggest Gregory might be marrying Penny for her future prospects? He could probably buy and sell the Blackwells from his petty cash.

Gregory stuck out his hand. "I appreciate your coming in on such short notice, Brad." He motioned to the chairs that were arranged in front of his desk. "Won't you have a seat?"

"I don't mind. I haven't been all that booked up this week," Brad said casually.

"I'm sure that Penny has kept you company during your convalescence."

Brad tried to read something into that statement—sarcasm, anger, jealousy. He heard none of those things. It had been a simple statement. Brad looked at the older man who had seated himself behind the desk once more. "Yes, she has." He raised one brow slightly. "Does that bother you?"

"To the contrary," Gregory said with a brief smile. "I fully expected to hear it, which is why I called you. There's something I need to say to you."

Feeling as though he were in the middle of a play and had forgotten his lines, Brad waited for Gregory to continue.

Gregory leaned his arms on the desk blotter lying in front of him, clasped his hands and met Brad's gaze with his own. "You're in love with Penny, aren't you?"

He'd been right. Gregory was going to see that he was removed from Penny's life. Brad wished he found the situation a little more amusing. How could he convince the man that his love for Penny was the very thing that would prevent him from doing anything to hurt her marriage to Gregory? Searching for the right words, Brad finally shrugged and admitted, "Yes, I am, but you're the man she's marrying."

"No, I'm not," Gregory replied quietly.

Brad was convinced something was wrong with his hearing. Perhaps the blow to his head had... "I beg your pardon?"

"You heard me."

"Of course you're marrying Penny. The rehearsal is tonight and tomorrow—"

"Tomorrow I will be in California. I discovered earlier today where a key witness is located. I'm flying out tonight to take his deposition."

"But the wedding?"

Gregory leaned back. "Ah, yes, the wedding." He placed his hands behind his head. "An interesting situation, isn't it? Two men who love Penny, discussing a wedding that isn't going to come off.''

"Couldn't you postpone your deposition or whatever? Surely Penny is more important than—''

"I understand your concern. Now you need to understand mine. I've had a great deal of time to think this week and I've come to the conclusion that Penny seriously misled me.''

"What are you talking about? Penny doesn't lie!''

"Please don't put words in my mouth,'' Gregory responded.

Brad was now facing the courtroom lawyer and recognized he could be a formidable foe.

"When I met Penny I thought she was everything I wanted in a wife. Since then I've come to know her better, and I've had reason to revise that opinion.''

"What's that supposed to mean?''

"I've decided that marrying Penny would be a mistake on my part.''

"Why?'' Brad demanded to know.

"For over a year I've spent time with the quiet, organized, unflappable woman I knew as Penny Blackwell. Yet in three days a volatile, passionate woman I never knew existed emerged as a result of your presence. I'm not comfortable with that person. I have no room for her in my life.'' He nodded to the younger man. "I believe I have you to thank for the transformation. As far as I'm concerned, I've had a very narrow escape.''

Brad came to his feet. "That's a hell of a thing to say! You wait until the day before your wedding to decide you don't know the woman you intend to marry so you're backing out? How can you do this to Penny? When do you intend to tell her how you feel?"

"I don't."

Brad had never felt such a murderous rage in all of his life. Gregory was calmly explaining that he intended to destroy Penny's life without even bothering to warn her?

"You really are a no-good, son-of-a—"

"Yes, I probably am. However, I did not reach my age or gain the experience I presently possess by being quixotic and foolish. I don't believe Penny understands what it is she feels for me. Whatever she feels, I don't think it's what I want from my wife. It's better to make a clean break now."

Gregory watched the younger man as though evaluating his reaction to what he'd just been told.

He got an immediate response. "You really are cold-blooded, aren't you? You don't care what you do to Penny, how you hurt her. She didn't measure up to some ridiculous standards you seem to have, so you're going to abandon her at the church."

"I don't intend to be that dramatic. I'll leave that sort of thing to you. You seem well-trained for it."

"If you don't intend telling her you've changed your mind, how the hell is she going to know?"

Gregory met his gaze and deliberately smiled. "Why, you'll tell her, of course. Why do you suppose I asked you to come in today?"

"Me? Are you out of your mind? It isn't my place to—"

"You're her friend, aren't you?"

"You're damn right I'm her friend, but—"

"I'm sure she'd rather receive such news from you."

"You're wrong! She'd rather hear it from you!"

"Somehow, I doubt that very much," Gregory said in a dry voice.

"Well, of course, you're right. Nobody wants to be told on the eve of their wedding that the other party has backed out."

"I have to agree."

"But it's none of my business. This is between you and Penny," Brad protested.

"Not any longer. I am here only long enough to pick up some papers I need. I'm leaving as soon as we're through here. How you want to handle everything from now on is up to you."

"Well, thank you very much. For nothing. How in the hell can I help her face this?"

Gregory rubbed his chin thoughtfully. "You could always take my place at the church tomorrow."

Chapter Six

By the time Brad reached home his head felt as though it were going to explode. He didn't even remember leaving Gregory Duncan's office or driving home. Only the intense pain in his head held his attention until he realized he was sitting in his room, staring at the wall.

He had to find Penny and tell her. But how was he going to break the news? Damn the man, anyway. How could anyone be so unfeeling as to walk out on someone the day before the wedding?

It would break Penny's heart.

Forcing himself to go in search of her, Brad started through the kitchen of his home.

"Your head must be really bothering you," his

mother said when she saw his expression. "Why don't you lie down and rest awhile?"

He turned, wincing at the sudden movement. "I've got to talk to Penny."

"She should be over here before much longer. Why don't you rest until she gets here?"

Perhaps that was good advice. He would take some of the pain medication the doctor had given him when he left the hospital. He hadn't used it before, but at the moment he was willing to do whatever he could for some relief.

After swallowing the tablets he stretched out on the bed and waited for Penny to come.

Oh, God, Penny. If only you didn't have to go through all of this.

By the time Penny peeked in to see if he still wanted to play chess, she found him sound asleep. His mother had told her that he had gone out for a while and was concerned that he had tried to do too much, too soon. She mentioned that he wanted to see Penny, but they both agreed it would be better to leave him alone and let him rest.

Penny had enough on her mind. She hadn't talked with Gregory since Monday evening, which wasn't like him at all. And he hadn't called to let her know he was back today. What if he was late for the rehearsal, or even worse, unable to make it?

She wouldn't let herself think of that. If he was delayed too much, she was certain he would call. Gregory was an honorable man and dependable. If she hadn't been in such a turmoil all week she wouldn't have worked herself up to such a state now.

Everything was under control. She would see Gregory this evening and they could laugh at her silliness.

Her mother decided not to go to the rehearsal so Penny drove to the church alone. Her dad was coming directly from his office.

When everyone was there but Gregory, Reverend Wilder suggested they begin. "After all, the groom has very little to do. I think that's for a reason," he kidded. "Usually the groom is too nervous to think of much of anything."

They all laughed politely, then followed his instructions.

"Have you talked with Gregory today?" Penny's father asked while they waited their turn to go down the aisle.

"No, I haven't."

"I hope nothing is wrong."

"So do I. Perhaps he just got held up. He's probably on his way now."

"Well, he could have called to let you know."

She gave her father a sidelong glance. "You know, Dad, that thought *had* crossed my mind."

He chuckled and patted her arm. "I'm sorry. I suppose I'm more nervous about the groom's absence than you are."

"Not necessarily. But I don't want anyone to think I'm nervous. What you are presently witnessing is my superb acting ability."

At that moment Reverend Wilder motioned for them to start down the aisle. Penny and her father didn't have a chance to speak in private again.

When Brad woke up he noted with relief that his head felt considerably better. Then he noticed it was dark. "Oh, no!" His sudden effort to sit up on the bed reminded him that he was far from being cured, despite the rest.

By the time he got over to the Blackwells', he knew he'd missed Penny. Helen confirmed his guess. "If you want to see her, you're welcome to wait. I'm sure they'll be home soon."

Brad was too restless at the moment to sit and try to make conversation. What he had to tell Penny had to be said in private. What she chose to do after that was anybody's guess. But it wasn't up to him to inform her mother or anyone else.

Brad spent the next few hours rehearsing what he needed to say to Penny.

"You could always marry her yourself," Gregory had said. The refrain kept running over and over through Brad's head.

There was just one thing wrong with that idea. Penny had no desire to marry him. She was in love with Gregory Duncan. The louse. The no-good, rotten arrogant fool who didn't care that he was leaving her to face the embarrassment and humiliation of a church full of people and no bridegroom.

What was she going to do at this late date? How could she possibly call everyone and explain? What could she say? How could Gregory Duncan have done such a thing to her? If he had any feelings for her at all, he would have talked to her, either in person or even by telephone. At the very least, he could have written her.

Why the hell had he chosen Brad to break the news to her?

That's what friends are for. Was that it? Gregory knew that Brad would do his best to shield Penny as much as possible. He'd even marry her if it would help.

Brad thought about that for a long while. Would it help? It couldn't make things any worse. At least she could have the wedding as planned, the reception. He seriously doubted she'd be interested in a honeymoon. Not with him, anyway. Brad tried not to allow himself to think about a honeymoon where he and Penny would be together, alone, and legally married. That way of thinking led to insanity.

Perhaps he and Penny could work out something so that she wouldn't feel abandoned and forgotten. She would never have a need to feel that way as long as Brad was around.

Ralph and Penny got home at about the same time. Her mother said that Brad had been looking for her. There had been no message from Gregory.

She glanced at the time. It was almost eleven—too late to see what Brad wanted. Her parents went up to bed, knowing they would need their rest for the next day.

Penny almost called Brad anyway. She needed to talk to someone. Not just someone, she needed Brad, she realized. He was the only person she knew with whom she could share her fears and be sure he wouldn't laugh.

But his mother said he was still suffering from considerable pain. No doubt he was already asleep now, and he really needed his rest.

Oh, well. She'd see him at the reception tomorrow, and they could chat before she and Gregory left to go wherever it was that Gregory planned to take her. Once Brad returned to New York, Penny knew her life would resume its normal pace.

She knew that he wasn't to blame for all her restlessness this week, but he seemed to symbolize a certain freedom that she was willingly giving up by marrying Gregory. She knew she'd feel more at peace once Brad wasn't around to remind her.

Quietly climbing the stairs, Penny went into her room and without turning on the light grabbed her nightshirt and went into her bathroom. She went through her nightly ritual, showering and drying her hair. Tonight she needed to remember to soak her contacts. She wouldn't want to be bothered next week while they were traveling. Thank God she knew the way to bed blindfolded, she thought with a grin. It was amazing how dependent she'd become on her extended-wear lenses.

Flipping off the light she felt her way to the bed and had almost reached it when a hand touched her arm and a voice said, "Don't let me scare—"

She was already beginning to scream when a hand clamped over her mouth in a firm grip.

"Oh, for God's sake, Penny. I'm not a rapist! What's the matter with you?"

As soon as she heard his voice, she recognized Brad but she hadn't been able to control her involuntary scream. She went limp in his arms and he released her mouth.

"Are you okay? I didn't hurt you, did I?" he asked in a low voice. Brad reached over to the bedside lamp and turned it on. They both blinked in the sudden light.

"How did you get in here?" she hissed.

"The same way I always got into your room—through the window, remember?" He motioned to the opened window and the oak tree that stood outside.

"What is so important that you have to scare me half out of my mind to tell me? Couldn't it have waited until tomorrow?" She wished she could focus on his face better. Penny couldn't see his expression at all. She sat down on the edge of the bed and glared at him.

"You're wearing my old football jersey," Brad said in a wondering tone.

"You mean you risked your neck climbing that old tree to crawl into my window to tell me that?" she asked incredulously.

"Of course not. I just didn't know you had kept it, that's all."

She sighed. "I kept every one you gave me. I find them very comfortable to sleep in. I've used them for years."

He couldn't help grinning but she didn't seem to notice. Now that he looked more closely, she didn't seem to be looking at him. At least, she was staring at him, but she didn't see him. She had that same vague, unfocused look she used to get when... "You don't have your contacts in, do you?" he asked, suddenly comprehending why she seemed somehow different.

Penny began to feel bewildered. Brad didn't seem to be his normal self at all, tonight. Then she remembered, But, of course; he was still recovering from his accident. That blow to the head might have caused more serious damage than anyone had realized.

Oh, how horrible! Maybe there had been some brain damage that was only now beginning to be apparent. Penny got up from the bed and walked over to him. Touching his arm she said in a calm, soothing voice. "That's right, Brad. I have to soak them once a week to keep them clean of protein buildup."

Leading him over to the bed, she coaxed him to sit down. She sat beside him and patted his hand.

"I'm really pleased that you came to see me tonight, Brad. I'm sorry I didn't get a chance to visit with you these past couple of days." She glanced up at him with concern. "I suppose your head still really bothers you."

Brad looked at her and had an almost uncontrollable urge to reach out and haul her into his arms. There she was, looking so concerned about him and his problems, unaware of what was happening in her life.

He loved her so much. She deserved better treatment, she really did. If he hadn't been so shocked when Gregory had informed him of his intentions, Brad would have loved to have laid him out. Let Mr. Duncan appear in California to take depositions with a lovely shiner! He deserved more than that.

Penny stroked his brow, subtly checking to see if he was feverish. "Why don't you go home now and get some rest. We're both tired." She smiled. "It wouldn't do for the bride to be drawn and wan tomorrow, you know."

He flinched at her words, grateful she couldn't see him any better. Otherwise she would read the distress that was obvious on his face.

"Yes, well, that's what I wanted to talk to you about, Penny," Brad finally managed to mumble.

His voice sounded so soft and hesitant, which only increased Penny's alarm. He didn't sound at all like himself. Oh, if only she'd taken the time to check on him during the past couple of days. But he'd seemed to be improving. His mother hadn't reported anything out of the ordinary. What could have happened to have brought on these dismaying symptoms?

"You want to talk about tomorrow, Brad?" she questioned as casually as possible.

"Yes."

She waited a moment, but he didn't say anything more. Finally, she said, "Okay."

Brad sat there, staring at her, remembering all of their shared time together. He'd lost track of how often he'd climbed the tree outside her window and sneaked into her room. She had been just as bad about using the tree as an escape to meet him somewhere.

The innocence of youth. It had not occurred to either of them that there was anything wrong with them shinnying in and out of each other's bedroom windows. It had been a game. Some of their greatest adventures had been planned while sitting on one of their beds cross-legged, letting their imaginations fly before them like kites in the sky.

Brad admitted to himself that he felt different now. He was well aware that they were no longer children. Even with her face freshly scrubbed and her hair brushed into submission, Penny could scarcely pass as a child. His old football jersey did not disguise her womanly form or hide her well-shaped legs. Brad felt such a strong surge of love for her that it set him trembling.

How dare Gregory Duncan hurt her—his wonderful, lovable, gentle Penny. She never harmed anyone; she only saw the good in everyone. Even now, Penny had complete trust and faith in the man who was too cowardly to tell her he wasn't going to marry her tomorrow.

"What about tomorrow?" Penny prodded gently, wondering if she should slip out and try to get one or the other sets of parents. Maybe they should take him to the emergency room tonight. Perhaps something suddenly had come loose inside his head, causing his rather strange and unusual behavior.

"The wedding," he managed to say, desperately seeking the right words to tell her.

"That's right, Brad," she said in the same soothing tone she'd been using for several minutes, "Tomorrow is the wedding. And I'm getting married."

"No, you're not," he said baldly.

Oh, dear. He was getting more and more irrational.

"I'm not?"

"No."

"I see. Why am I not getting married?"

She sounded so calm, as though she were humoring him. Of course she'd been under a great deal of strain this week, herself. "Because Gregory isn't going to marry you." There. He'd told her. He waited for her reaction. He knew the rest of the night was going to be hell. At first she'd try to deny it. That was only to be expected. Then she'd probably cry, and get angry—the anger would help, he decided. He would stay with her through all of it, and whatever she decided to do in the morning, he'd agree. If she wanted him to marry her, he would. That's what friends are for, after all, to help in a time of crisis.

What he hadn't expected was her calm acceptance. "Why isn't Gregory going to marry me?" she asked casually.

"Why?" he repeated, not knowing what to say.

"Um-hmm."

"Oh. Well. It has something to do with me, I think. I'm not sure."

"Brad, are you still feeling guilty because you intended to break up our engagement?" she asked with sudden inspiration and understanding. She put her arms around his waist and lovingly laid her head on his chest. "Oh, you poor darling. That's what we were discussing just before the accident. It must have been haunting you all week." She glanced up, unable to see the glazed look in his eyes. "Brad, love, I have forgiven you for that. Please try to understand. No one is going to hold your intentions against you. After all, you changed your mind. And you were even concerned enough to tell me, which I appreciated, very much." Placing her head back on his chest she continued, "Now I want you to go home and get some rest, okay? I appreciate your coming over tonight, I really do. But I don't want you worrying about anything, you hear me?"

She could feel his heart pounding in his chest, like a bird beating its wings against a cage. Penny felt like crying. There was no telling what was going through his poor, confused mind at the moment. Whatever it was, he was concerned about her. No matter what he was suffering, he was still thinking of her.

"Penny!" he said in a strangled voice, "You don't understand!"

She raised her head and kissed him lightly on the lips. Surely Gregory would understand why she would be kissing another man the night before her wedding. The kiss was meant only to comfort. She had to do whatever it took to calm Brad down until they could get some help for him.

His arms came around her convulsively and he hung on to her like a drowning man. During all the hours he had agonized over how to tell her, how much to tell her, never had Brad envisioned that she wouldn't believe him.

He couldn't understand why not. Was her faith in Gregory Duncan so strong that the only proof she would accept would be entering the church in the morning and finding no groom waiting?

She felt so small against him, and she was so vulnerable. Penny had no idea what she had to face tomorrow, unless he took Gregory's advice and became the substitute bridegroom.

Is that why Gregory had told him, instead of her? Was he giving Brad the option of marrying her, himself?

How could he explain to her? "Penny?"

"Hmm?"

"I love you."

She smiled, her head resting on his shoulder. "I'm so glad."

"No. I really mean it. I want to marry you."

Her head jerked up and she stared at him, truly concerned. "Oh, Brad, please don't talk that way."

"I mean it. Gregory won't marry you, but I will."

"Oh, Brad. Please don't do this to either one of us. Please. It's too late for us. Don't you understand that? Maybe if we'd had this discussion before you left for New York everything would have worked out differently." She pulled back slightly and placed her hands on his neck, cupping his jawline. "You can never go back, Brad, no matter what. Perhaps if I hadn't met Gregory, and I'd known how you feel about me..." She paused, wanting him to understand, not wanting to cause him any more grief. "It's too late for us," she finished softly.

"No, it isn't. Believe me, it isn't."

She just shook her head. "Oh, Brad. If only life weren't so complicated." She slipped off the bed and stood in front of him. "Go home, now, Brad. We'll meet tomorrow and pretend this conversation never took place. It's just between you and me, like so many other things that we've shared together."

Brad sat there staring at her. He'd tried to tell her. In fact, he had told her, but for whatever reason, she hadn't believed him. His options at this point were severely limited.

The question was, what would she do tomorrow when she discovered that Gregory wasn't there? Would she allow him to substitute for the missing groom?

Knowing Penny the way he did, he sincerely doubted it. In the first place, she would assume he was doing it out of pity for her because of the humiliation she would suffer. Pity had nothing to do with the feelings he had for this woman.

But he needed time to explain, time to make her understand. And from the looks of things tonight, she wasn't going to listen to what he had to say. She'd been under considerable strain all week. He knew that. Stress could have a strange effect on people.

Feeling a wealth of love for the woman who stood in front of him, Brad made up his mind. He would do whatever he had to do to protect her from a situation not of her own making.

Brad stood and smiled down at her. "Everything's going to be all right, love. I'll take care of it."

She nodded, glad to see that he appeared to be calming down.

He turned and pulled back the covers, helping her as though she were an invalid. Docilely she went along with him. There was no reason to upset him. He certainly wasn't dangerous to anyone—just a little irrational. Hopefully that would pass in a few hours. Surely it wouldn't take more than a few days to help him recover. Penny prayed his condition wouldn't be permanent.

"I'll get you a glass of water," he announced as though coming up with a brilliant idea. "That should help you sleep." He turned away and disappeared into her bathroom. She heard the water running, and he eventually reappeared.

"It will?" she asked, wondering if he had water confused with warm milk.

He carefully handed her a glass filled with water. Penny smiled and took it, dutifully taking a sip.

"Now don't worry about a thing, do you hear me?" Brad asked in an urgent tone. "Everything's going to work out just fine. You know I'll always take care of you."

"Yes," she agreed, nodding.

Brad leaned over and touched her lips softly with his. "I think I'll let myself out the back door rather than go down the tree, if that's all right," he suggested.

"Oh, yes! I wouldn't want you to slip and fall, for heaven's sake. You've had enough bumps to your head for one week!"

They smiled at each other, pleased that they had reached some sort of harmonious understanding.

Penny listened until she heard the faint sound of the back door closing, then sighed and turned out the light.

Now not only did she have to worry about whether or not the groom would show up for his wedding in the morning, she also had to live with the fear that her best friend might have received some sort of brain damage that had gone undetected until now.

Chapter Seven

Good morning, darling," Helen said to her sleeping daughter. "I thought I'd bring you coffee in bed this morning, since it will be the last time you'll be here with us."

Penny rolled over onto her back and groggily looked up at her mother. She could see that her mother was trying not to cry at the thought that her daughter was leaving home at long last. Too bad she couldn't appreciate that very few women continued to live at home until they were twenty-five, Penny thought with amusement.

She pushed herself up, propping her pillow against the headboard. "Thanks, Mom," she said, sipping the coffee, then holding the cup between her hands.

Her mother sank onto the end of the bed. "I'm being so ridiculous, acting like this, when I've known for months you were leaving."

Penny grinned. "That's true, but I understand. I suppose I feel a little weepy myself."

"However, I'm extremely happy for you, Penny. You know I was always a little concerned before. I'm so glad you decided to go ahead and follow your heart after all, no matter what," Helen said, her face radiant. "I want you to know how proud I am of you."

Penny stared at her mother in confusion. What in the world was she talking about? Follow her heart? She shook her head. It was too early in the morning to try to work out word games.

Helen stood, leaned over and kissed her. "Breakfast will be ready in a few minutes, dear. I know you're excited, but you'll need to eat something before we leave for the church."

"I know, Mom."

Her mother smiled at her from the doorway. "It's hard to believe it. My fondest wish is finally coming true."

Penny stared blankly at the door. Her fondest wish? Had her mother secretly coveted her room for some reason? Why else would she suddenly be so pleased while at the same time lamenting that Penny was leaving home today?

She shrugged. Maybe the excitement of the wedding was getting to her mother. She usually seemed very sane and sensible.

Penny discovered that her father wasn't making much sense, either. He came bounding into the kitchen while she was struggling to eat the breakfast her mother had prepared and gave her a big hug. "My God, Penny! You are simply wonderful. I still can't believe it. I'm so proud of you. I'm not losing a daughter, I'm finally gaining the son I've always wanted."

She watched as he poured himself a cup of coffee and joined her at the table.

"I still find it hard to believe," Ralph said with a wide grin. "The two of you are actually getting married this morning. Unbelievable!"

Perhaps her dad had been in some sort of time warp during the past few months. Otherwise he wouldn't find the idea of her wedding day quite so unbelievable. Although he had always been polite and cordial to Gregory, Penny had never heard her father express such a strong sentiment toward him before. She was pleased to see him warming to the idea.

Penny and her bridesmaids planned to change into their dresses at the church, so all she had to do before leaving home was her makeup and hair. After dutifully eating her breakfast, Penny took her time returning upstairs. She had plenty of time before they had to leave.

After a few moments in the bathroom, she hurried to her bedroom door, trying not to panic. "Mom!"

"Yes, dear," Helen responded from downstairs, a lilt to her voice.

"I hate to bother you, but I can't seem to find my contacts," she said, walking out into the hallway. Her mother came up the stairs and Penny went on, consciously working to stay calm. "I know they were here last night. I soaked them overnight but they aren't where I thought I left them." She turned back into her room.

Her mother followed her and walked over to the bathroom. "I'm not surprised. You were probably so caught up in all the excitement you didn't pay any attention to where you set them down."

"I wish I weren't so blind," Penny muttered. How many times had she said that, or thought it, over the years? She followed her mother into the smaller room, feeling frustrated and helpless. Her mother began to move items around on the countertop, then peeked into the cabinets above the sink.

"Find them?" Penny asked, hopefully.

Helen looked around, puzzled. "Are you sure you took them out? Because I don't see them anywhere."

"Of course I'm sure, Mom. I left them in their soaking solution. Believe me, I know when I've got them in or not."

Helen shook her head. "Well, they aren't here, Penny."

Penny could feel the surge of panic she'd been holding at bay sweep over her. "What do you mean they aren't there?" she cried. "They have to be! Maybe they got knocked off onto the floor." She immediately fell to her knees and began to feel around on the smooth surface. Helen joined her until they had covered every square inch of the bathroom floor.

"They aren't here, Penny," Helen said finally, stating the obvious. She and Penny stared at each other, nose to nose on the bathroom floor. The enormity of the missing contacts settled over them slowly.

"What am I going to do?" Penny asked in a pleading voice, begging for reassurance.

"I don't know." Helen pushed herself up and looked around the room, as if hoping the contacts would suddenly appear before her. "Perhaps you could wear your glasses?"

"Oh, Mother," Penny wailed, almost in tears, "I haven't had the prescription changed in years." She walked into her bedroom and glanced around wildly. "I don't even know where they are!" She sank down on the side of the bed, her face in her hands. "Oh, dear God. What am I going to do?"

Helen sat down beside her daughter. "Well, you're not going to panic, for starters. So what if you can't see very well?" she said briskly, making it sound as though Penny was worrying over a hangnail. "We'll call for another set to be made up for you and have them mailed to you. You'll probably only have to do without them for a few days."

"But what about today?"

Helen could see that her daughter was about to fall apart. Poor dear. So many things had been happening to her and she'd handled them all so well. Now here she was going to pieces over such a little thing. But not if Helen could help it.

"I'll do your face and hair and help you dress." She laughed and went on, "And your dad is going to walk you down the aisle. After that you can use your brand-new husband as a Seeing Eye dog for a day or two. I have a feeling he won't mind in the least!"

What a way to start a marriage. And why hadn't she ever ordered an extra set of contacts? Of all days to lose hers. And what in the world had she done with them? She couldn't imagine, but then, she'd been so distracted last night. For all she knew she might have put them in her cold cream or skin freshener!

Penny tried not to let the missing contacts cast a pall over her preparations. At least she could see shapes and wouldn't walk into any walls or doors. Her mother and dad seemed to be in high enough spirits to make up for any lack on her part. If she didn't know better, she would think they'd already gotten into the champagne.

Time seemed to speed up once they arrived at the church. There was a great deal of laughing and teasing among all of her friends while they dressed, and later, one or more would dash back in to report the swelling crowd. The church seemed to be filled to capacity.

Before she left home, Penny had slipped away long enough to call Gregory's house. There had been no answer. Of course he might have left early, even gone to the office for a final check. There was even the possibility that he had been held up in St. Louis and was even now driving back to be there on time.

But why hadn't he called her?

Penny knew that she could have her fears allayed by simply asking someone if Gregory had arrived, but after the teasing about the missing groom she'd received the night before, she wouldn't give them the satisfaction of knowing that she was worried.

Anyway, she would know soon enough. They certainly wouldn't be able to start without him.

So she waited, trying to be calm. This was her wedding day. The day she had looked forward to for months. The reason that Brad had—

Brad! She had forgotten to tell her parents about his strange behavior the night before! Oh, how could she have forgotten? She'd been so wrapped up in herself that his problems had completely slipped her mind. If his parents hadn't noticed, perhaps she was the only one who could sound a warning...

The door to the room where she waited swung open and Penny could hear the organ music. She heard a voice speaking to the congregation, then a burst of laughter and applause. What in the world?

Her father hurried through the door, a wide grin on his face. "You look beautiful, my darling daughter. Just beautiful. Are you ready to go?"

"Uh, yes. Is everything... I mean, are we all...?"

"Yes, everything's moving on schedule." He took her arm and gave it a squeeze as he escorted her into the foyer to wait their turn. "You have made me a very happy man, you know that, don't you?"

At least her father was making no effort to hide his elation at finally getting rid of his daughter, she decided with wry amusement. "I'm glad," she said softly.

"I just couldn't see you with— No. This isn't the place. I'm just happy that you made the right choice."

The right choice? More cryptic comments. Had it only now occurred to her father that she could have moved in with Gregory first, before the wedding? He needn't have worried. Her upbringing would have prevented her from even entertaining the idea and Gregory had seemed content to wait for all the legalities before he claimed her.

She had no more time to think about her father's remark. Suddenly the music stopped and everyone in the church stood. The slow, stately march began, signaling that it was time for her entrance.

For the first time Penny was grateful she couldn't see more clearly. She was having an awful attack of stage fright, which was absolutely ridiculous. Crowds had never bothered her before. She'd found excitement on the stage. However, always before this she was playing someone else. Today she was Penelope Anne Blackwell and she wasn't at all sure she could make it down the aisle without tripping or in some way making a fool of herself.

She forced herself to take a calming breath, then began to take the slow, gliding steps they had rehearsed the night before.

The light from the stained glass window fell on Gregory's blond hair and Penny suddenly let go of the breath she unconsciously had been holding. He had come. He was here.

She began to smile. Everything was all right. All the last minute details had worked out. And the groom had managed to show up when he was needed. Penny began to plan some of the things she was going to say to him once they were alone. What a scare he'd given her!

When she got close enough Penny saw Reverend Wilder standing before her, smiling. At least she assumed it was he. The man appeared to be the right height and size for it. When she and her father paused she noticed that Gregory stepped beside her and faced the altar with her.

Reverend Wilder's melodious voice filled the sanctuary with the age-old ceremonial words of the wedding vows. Tears began to collect in her eyes at the beauty of the vows they were sharing.

Then the dream seemed to dissolve into a nightmare.

She heard Reverend Wilder say, "Do you, Bradley Aaron Crawford, take this woman—"

Bradley Aaron Crawford? *Bradley Aaron Crawford!* Penny turned her head and stared at the man standing beside her, the man she was in the process of marrying. There was a small white patch gleaming on his left temple.

Brad.

She never clearly remembered anything that happened during the rest of the ceremony. She must have made the right responses since no one seemed to find anything out of the ordinary in the situation. Perhaps it was only her; obviously she was suffering from some sort of delusion, she decided, dazed. Although she'd been convinced she was engaged to Gregory Duncan, she was marrying Brad Crawford.

"I now pronounce you man and wife," Reverend Wilder intoned. "You may kiss the bride."

Slowly Penny turned to the man she had just married. He carefully and tenderly lifted the veil from her face and folded it neatly back, then leaned down to kiss her.

"What are you doing here!" she whispered through barely moving lips.

He smiled and lightly kissed her on the mouth. "Marrying you," he replied as he straightened to his full height.

The triumphant music from the organ filled the large room and the entire audience stood and clapped their welcome to the new couple.

Penny wished she were the fainting type. What a wonderful way that would be to get out of an intolerable situation.

Brad swept her down the aisle, out into the foyer and into a private room. Closing the door, he reached into his pocket and pulled out something. "Here."

She blinked and peered into his hand. "What is it?"

"Your contact lenses."

"My contact lenses?" she repeated stupidly, wondering how he had known she hadn't been able to find them. And then the truth seemed to drop on her like a sudden resounding crash of boulders. "You?" she said, desperately trying to make some sense out of her whirling thoughts and emotions. A rage such as she had not felt in years took control of her. "You—

Bradley Aaron Crawford—*you* took my contacts? You hid them from me, knowing I would be blind without them?"

He nodded. "I needed every advantage I could think of. You made it clear last night that if I gave you any warning, you'd refuse to allow me to help you, to save you from the embarrassment of having to call off the wedding."

"What are you talking about? Have you lost your mind?" she demanded. Then hearing her own words, things began to make a twisted sort of sense.

"Of course," she said, pacing, her long train trailing behind her, "That's it! You had that terrible blow to the head and now you've—"

She stopped suddenly and spun around, almost losing her balance in all the satin and lace material that wrapped around her when she turned. She gazed at him, her eyes widening with growing horror. "Gregory! You've done something to him. What did you do, Brad?" She fought the entangling folds of her dress and rushed over to him. Grabbing his arms and trying to shake him she yelled, "What have you done with Gregory, Brad? Answer me!"

"Penny, calm down! I haven't done anything to Gregory Duncan. Don't be so damned dramatic."

"Dramatic! Me? Why, I couldn't begin to compare with you, you no-good, rotten, egotistical louse. Just how much more dramatic did you intend to get? You managed to spirit away my fiancé in some way so you could take his place!"

Once again she began to pace, gathering her dress in both hands and bundling the folds in front of her, as though acting out a scene of a primitive washer-woman striding around the room with her load of clothes.

"Well, I won't stand for it, do you hear me?" Her voice continued to grow in volume. "I have had it with you, do you understand? I have taken all I intend to take from you and your stupid, idiotic pranks! You did your best to ruin my childhood by scaring me with snakes, putting frogs in my bed, hiding my glasses—"

"Damn it! I've told you and told you—I never did a thing to your stupid glasses. Even your mother believed me when I told her I had nothing to do with your losing them!"

She ignored the interruption. "You'd invite me to play with you, then run off and hide so nobody knew where you were, and then you would laugh because I cried when I couldn't find you!"

"Come on, Penny," he said, "be reasonable! That was twenty years ago, for God's sake!"

By now she was caught up in remembering all the many grievances she had against him. Ignoring his comment Penny continued going down her list. "And what about that time when we were in high school, how mortified I was by your absolutely awful teasing in front of Frank Tyler when you knew I had a crush on him!"

"Hey, Runt, you held your own in that department and you know it! How many girls did you tell your ridiculous stories about me so they'd never take me seriously!''

"Take you seriously? You? The original good-time man-about-town? You've never taken anything seriously in your whole life! It's all been fun and games for you, all the times we were growing up, and even when we went away to college.''

She stopped pacing and stared at him from across the room, her face flushed and angry. "I was never so glad when you moved to New York and out of my life, do you hear me? Every time you're around crazy things happen. Nothing ever works out the way I plan. It was only after you were gone that I finally managed to get some order in my life and find the man I loved and intended to marry and then you—'' The enormity of what had just taken place swept over her like a tidal wave and she began to cry, harsh sobs that shook her body. "No-w-w...yo-you've...com-completely...ruined...m-my life!''

Brad could only stand there and watch her. He had honestly thought he was helping her out. He certainly had no intention of ruining her life. He loved her. He had only wanted to help her... or so he had managed to convince himself when he decided to substitute himself for Gregory at the altar.

Who are you kidding, Crawford? he asked himself. *You've been eating your heart out every day since you learned she was marrying someone else.* When he'd seen his opportunity, he'd grabbed it, using Gregory's desertion to finally get what he wanted.

And Penny hated him for it.

Brad could feel the guilt churn in his stomach. He'd managed to make her his wife, but at what price? What could he possibly do or say that would ever help her forgive him?

Slowly he walked over to her and reached out his hand. She jerked away as if she found the mere thought of his touching her repulsive. He dropped his hand and just looked at her.

Penny fought for control, trying to get her breath. Through sobbing breaths she managed to grate out, "Where...is...Gregory?"

Brad sighed. He slid his hands into his pants pockets and turned away, gazing out the window.

"California."

"California? What's he doing out there?"

"Taking depositions."

She stared at him in disbelief. "You're making this up, aren't you? All of it? Gregory wouldn't have gone off like that, leaving me without some word."

Scrubbing at her face, Penny took a couple of breaths and forced herself into a semblance of calmness. "You warned me last Sunday," she said in a low voice that shook with the intensity of her hurt and rage. "You told me you had come back to break up the engagement! Too bad I didn't realize you were lying when you said you had changed your mind!"

"I wasn't lying, damn it!" he said, spinning on his heel to face her. "I've been telling you the truth!" Brad had finally been goaded beyond control.

"Well, if it wasn't a lie, what was it? You said you'd break us up. I'd say that substituting yourself for the groom certainly managed to do that! You don't care that Gregory and I already had our future planned together. You couldn't stand seeing me happy, could you? Well, Mr. Crawford, this time you managed to get caught in your own trap. Because you are just as married to me as I'm married to you. And I don't want to be married to you. I want Gregory!''

"You've made that good and clear. Believe me, there's nothing I'd rather see than you married to Gregory, damn it. Can't you understand that?"

She crossed her arms, her mutinous expression making it clear that she did not find his remarks appeasing.

"No, I can't understand it. Because you are here and he isn't."

"That isn't my fault."

"Isn't it?" she asked sarcastically.

"Listen to me, you hardheaded, obstinate shrew. If I hadn't married you, you would have been left here this morning having to explain to everybody who showed up why your groom begged off!"

His words were a verbal slap in the face and Penny flinched. "You mean that Gregory changed his mind?"

"That's exactly what I mean!"

"Why?"

"How the hell should I know?"

"He must have told you. Otherwise you wouldn't have known."

He nodded his head curtly. "He told me he had changed his mind. That he wasn't going to marry you.

He said something about not really knowing you as well as he thought."

The look she gave him was filled with contempt. "And you really expect me to believe that? There's absolutely no way of knowing what horrible lies you must have told him to cause him to change his mind about marrying me!"

"Stop calling me a liar!"

"Stop behaving like one!"

They had made no attempt to keep their voices down. In truth, the volume of the argument was the last thing they had considered. The sudden silence as they stood glaring at each other seemed to bounce off the walls of the room.

A soft tapping on the door made them look in that direction. "Come in," Brad commanded.

Helen stuck her head around the door and looked from one to the other in shocked dismay. She stepped inside and firmly closed the door behind her, leaning on it.

"I absolutely can't believe the two of you! You haven't been married five minutes and you already sound the way you used to as small children when your mother and I had to drag you apart and make you spend the day at home by yourselves until you could play together without fighting! Do you realize that you can be heard for a city block? Are you aware that the recreation hall is full of people waiting to greet the loving bride and groom and watch them open presents and cut their wedding cake?"

They immediately burst into simultaneous explanations.

"Mother, you don't understand. Brad—"

"Helen, she's being totally unreasonable and won't even listen to me!"

She put up her hand like a policeman stopping traffic. "I don't want to hear it! Thank goodness I no longer have to play referee for the two of you. If you choose to kill each other, you no longer have to explain it to me. Now I want you both to go over to that hall with smiles on your faces and show all those people how happy you are. They expect to see some sort of love and joy in the occasion."

"Love!" Penny repeated contemptuously.

"Joy!" Brad said with a harsh laugh.

Helen opened the door with a decisive turn of her wrist. "Both of you studied acting for years. Surely you have something to show for all the money we invested in your education." She looked at her watch. "I'm going over there and explain that you've been delayed. I'll expect to see your happy, smiling faces in no more than fifteen minutes."

Brad and Penny stared at the closed door for an unnoticed elapse of time after Helen left. Neither of them had any desire to look at the other.

Penny was the first one to break the silence. "What are we going to do?"

He glanced at her, then away, once again walking over to the window. "That's up to you, isn't it?"

"Why up to me?"

"You can go out there and tell everyone that you never intended to marry me."

"I don't understand why somebody didn't say something. I mean, everyone in the wedding party knew I was expecting Gregory to be here today."

"I told them that we talked it over late last night. You discovered that you couldn't marry Gregory after all . . . because you loved me."

"And they believed you?" she asked incredulously.

"Thanks a lot."

"You know what I mean. As mother just pointed out, you and I fight as much as we're friends."

"Your parents didn't seem to be as surprised as they were pleased."

Remembering their rather strange behavior she asked, "When did you tell them?"

"Early this morning, just as I told my parents. You probably didn't notice, but Dad was my best man."

She shook her head and looked down at the small container she held in her hands. "As you well know, I couldn't see anyone."

"I'm sorry. I had no right to hide your contacts from you."

"At least you admit it!"

"I was only trying to help."

"Fine, Brad. How do you propose to help now, go out there and announce the whole thing was a joke?"

"Hardly. Our marriage was very legal. We have the license to prove it."

"And that's another thing. How did you manage to get a license?"

"Well, one of the benefits of having been raised in a small town is knowing everybody, including the county clerk. It's amazing what people will do when they think they're assisting true love. I explained everything to Reverend Wilder and he made the announcement before the ceremony began, with a few comments about love conquering all."

So that was what she had heard just before her father escorted her down the aisle.

Penny sat down, feeling as though she were a balloon and someone had suddenly let out all of her air. "So Gregory didn't love me, after all," she said slowly. "He certainly had me fooled."

Brad heard the pain in her voice and could think of nothing to say.

"I should have known," she said, not even aware she had spoken aloud.

"What do you mean?"

"I hadn't talked to him all week. That isn't like him. Not at all. I kept telling myself he was just busy, but something kept nagging at me, a little voice that refused to shut up." She glanced up, then quickly away. "It's funny, really. I was just thinking last night that I wanted to discuss what I was feeling with you, knowing you'd understand." Looking down at her hands, she added, "Oh, you understood all right. I just wished you'd explained last night."

One corner of his mouth lifted in a half grin. "I tried, believe me. But you wouldn't accept what I said.

I didn't want to go into all the details, about Gregory calling me and what he said. When I realized that you weren't going to accept what I was saying, I guess I used the situation to my own advantage."

Penny didn't seem to hear his explanation or apologetic tone of voice. She had dropped her face in her hands. When he stopped speaking she cried, "I can't face all those people out there. I just can't."

"I could take you home and tell them you aren't feeling well."

The thought of returning home and trying to explain to her parents what had taken place was just as bad an idea as pretending to be happily married.

She looked over at Brad. "I don't think I'll ever forgive you for this ridiculous situation, but since you got us into this mess, I don't see anything else to do but go out there and pretend we're happy newlyweds."

"Happy?" he repeated sarcastically. "I don't think I'm that good an actor."

"What about me? At least you had a choice."

"So sue me!"

"Don't worry. I intend to just as soon as I know how to go about it."

He looked at her incredulously. "You mean you'd actually take me to court? On what grounds?"

"Don't be ridiculous. I don't want any money from you. I just meant I was going to end the marriage as soon as I know what to do."

"Oh."

She stood and began to brush the wrinkles out of the skirt of her gown. "I'm going to go put my contacts in so I can at least see who's here."

"I'll wait out in the hall for you. We need to arrive together, looking properly blissful."

Every time she thought of Brad's audacity she wanted to throw something at him. How was she going to be able to look at him with a loving smile all afternoon? She shook her head. Acting ability, indeed. It would be the performance of her life.

Penny went into the ladies' restroom and replaced her lenses. Being able to see helped to boost her morale somewhat. She stared at herself in the mirror. Her face was white and strained, her eyes slightly puffy. It was not the face of a typically blushing bride.

Their delay in joining everyone at the reception did not go unnoticed. As soon as they walked into the room everyone started clapping and some of the comments held sly innuendos of Brad's impatience to get her alone.

Oh, no, Penny thought. She'd forgotten all the jokes and teasing that went along with a wedding. The only way she was going to get through the afternoon was by shutting her mind to the fact that she was with the wrong man.

Her mother hurried them over near the table where a three-tiered cake sat waiting for them.

"You can stand here and receive everyone. Then the photographer will start posing you for pictures."

The photographer! Something else Penny had forgotten. She glanced at Brad, and unconsciously did a
double take.

She hadn't paid attention to him when she had come
out of the ladies' room. It was only now that she saw
what he looked like in his tuxedo.

He wore the traditional black and a ruffled shirt.
The clothes fit him as if tailored for his tall body with
its broad shoulders, lean hips, and long, muscular
legs. He looked magnificent. The dark suit enhanced
his tan and bright hair. The small bandage gave him a
rakish look that made him very appealing.

"Well, if you aren't the sly one, young lady," Mrs.
Fielding said, walking up and grabbing Penny's hand
in a firm grip. "Letting us think you were marrying
Mr. Duncan right up to the last minute. Of course you
never fooled me a bit, you know." She winked at
Brad. "But your engagement certainly served its purpose. It got Brad to come home so you two could work
everything out."

Penny couldn't look at Brad. She couldn't believe
the woman and she couldn't think of a thing to say in
reply to the outrageous comment.

Brad spoke up, sounding relaxed and nauseatingly
pleased with himself. "We're happy you and Mr.
Fielding could come today."

"Oh, we wouldn't have missed it for the world, even
before we knew of the dramatic denouement," she
said archly. "It must have to do with your theatrical
background and all."

Penny wondered how much longer she would be able to stand there and smile before she let out a scream.

"It was the most romantic thing I've ever seen," Mrs. Cantrell said when she reached them. "Why, when Reverend Wilder explained how you two suddenly realized how you felt about each other and that nice Mr. Duncan agreed to release you, I thought I would cry. It was better than anything I've ever seen on television!" She leaned over and whispered to Penny, "Even though he seemed a very nice man, I thought Mr. Duncan was too old for you anyway, dear. Isn't it nice how everything worked out so well?"

Penny wondered what all of these people would do if she suddenly started having hysterics? She felt very close to it at the moment. She had an absolutely insane urge to laugh and she knew the tears wouldn't be far behind. Already she could read the write-up in the local paper: "Bridegroom has to slap hysterical bride at wedding reception."

Somehow she managed to get through the next hour without breaking down. Then the photographer took over.

She would have been all right if she hadn't met Brad's eyes during one of the more soulful poses. The dancing light of amusement almost undid her. How many times had she seen the same expression on his face after they'd shared a joke?

Oh, Brad. No matter what, you manage to see the humor in every situation. Nothing in life ever really fazes you. How do you do it?

Then the photographer asked Brad to kiss her. This time the intent look in his eyes held a question. Taking a cue from him and determined not to treat what was happening like some gloomy Greek tragedy, Penny lifted her mouth and closed her eyes.

She felt his arms go around her and pull her tightly against him as his mouth found hers.

This kiss was nothing like the one he'd given her at the altar. As a matter of fact, it was like no other kiss he'd ever given her, and Brad had kissed her often over the years—friendly kisses, exuberant kisses, teasing kisses, hello kisses, goodbye kisses.

Penny couldn't compare this particular kiss with any of those. She felt a tingle in her body that started in her toes and shot up through her until she felt the top of her head seem to shoot off.

His lips felt firm yet they were also tender. He took his time, as though they had nothing better to do, as if there weren't a roomful of people watching and a photographer whose flash periodically added a fireworks display behind her closed eyelids.

Brad was kissing her the way he kissed the countless women Drew Derek pursued on television. No wonder they kept coming back for more!

Vaguely Penny became aware of the general laughter and a smattering of applause around them and she stiffened. They were making a spectacle of themselves.

She pushed herself away from him and glared up into his smiling face. "You're supposed to look happy," he said just under his breath, never breaking his smile.

Penny flashed him an equally brilliant smile. "You try that again and I will place my knee in the exact spot you instructed me to all those years ago to ward off unwanted advances!"

He flinched in mock horror. Then he laughed—he actually had the nerve to laugh. "To think that you would use my own teachings against me," he said, still too low for anyone to hear.

The photographer interrupted their murmured comments, convinced this was a couple who was counting the minutes until they could be alone. "Okay, now. How about some pictures with you both cutting the cake."

Why not? Penny thought. Maybe I can stuff enough cake into his mouth to choke him. "Bridegroom chokes to death on wedding cake." Then she remembered the previous Sunday's accident coming on the heels of her dire wishes for his early demise. Penny hurriedly explained to the Fates that she didn't really want him to die and to please ignore her last suggestion.

Opening the gifts brought back to her how differently this part of the afternoon would have gone if Gregory had been there instead. Brad seemed to be having a great deal of fun and the onlookers were relishing his reactions and comments.

She had to admit that his quick wit often caught her off guard and she found herself laughing at his humor and antics—until she picked up the envelope that must have fallen off one of the gifts. The envelope was addressed to Brad Crawford.

Very few people could have known that Brad would be there to open gifts. She handed the envelope to him in silence. When he opened it, Brad continued to stare down at the contents, his expression blank.

"Come on, Brad, don't hold out on us," someone yelled. "Somebody give you a million bucks?"

He glanced over at her and she noticed his color had faded.

"What is it?" she whispered.

Without a word he handed her two pieces of paper that looked like airline tickets. They were. She stared down at them in bewilderment. The tickets were for a round trip to Acapulco for Mr. and Mrs. Brad Crawford, leaving that afternoon from the airport nearest Payton, to return the following Saturday.

Penny looked up at Brad in dismay.

"Tell us! Tell us!" several people said, laughing.

Penny cleared her throat. "Well, it's, uh," she glanced at Brad helplessly. Brad looked at her and shrugged. She started again. "It's round-trip tickets to Acapulco, leaving in a few hours."

Her announcement created a great deal of excitement and speculation. "What a wonderful idea! Great wedding gift! Marvelous place for a honeymoon!"

Honeymoon? Penny's heart seemed to sink in her chest. She leaned over and whispered, "We can't use these. Who in the world gave them to us?"

"I don't think you want to know," he said, his expression deliberately noncommittal.

"What do you mean?"

He handed her a note that he had continued to hold. She stiffened when she saw the page with the name Gregory Duncan neatly imprinted at the top. His slashing handwriting read, "You might as well use these since they're paid for. The hotel reservations have been changed to your name." It was signed with Gregory's initials.

The realization of his betrayal seemed to flood over her and for a moment Penny thought she would double over with the pain. Brad must have recognized how she felt because he leaned over and said, "You know, Penny, it might not be a bad idea to take him up on the offer. It would give us time to get away and decide what to do. If we don't go, what then? All these people are just waiting to see us happily depart somewhere or another. Why not Acapulco?"

Acapulco. Gregory had remembered a conversation many months ago when she had commented that she had never been out of the United States. So that's where he'd planned to take her on their honeymoon.

What kind of man would leave his intended bride on the eve of her wedding, then provide the honeymoon trip as a wedding gift when she married someone else?

Penny realized that she didn't know Gregory Duncan at all. Perhaps she never had.

"What do you think?" Brad asked.

The problem was, she could no longer think. About anything. Everything had suddenly piled up on her and she felt that she couldn't deal with another decision. She looked at Brad and said, "I don't care at this point what we do or where we go. Just get me out of here.''

Taking her at her word, Brad used the tickets as a reason for their hurried departure. But the well-wishers couldn't let them leave without the traditional spray of rice over them as they dashed for Brad's mother's car.

''My suitcases!'' Penny gasped, hurrying down the sidewalk.

''Your dad said he put them into my car this morning.''

They got into the car, waving at all the happy, smiling people who had helped them to celebrate their wedding day.

Brad took Penny's hand and squeezed it gently, then placed it on his thigh before driving away. ''Well, Mrs. Crawford. We may have the shortest marriage in history, but it looks like we're going to have our honeymoon!''

Chapter Eight

Penny stood on the balcony of the luxury hotel and stared at the sun as it set over the Pacific. She had never seen the ocean before and knew that she should be experiencing all of the excitement of the unknown.

The view below had all the earmarks of a fantasy— white sands, gently swaying palm trees, and the variegated blues of the ocean—a virtual tropical paradise.

Penny felt no excitement, no anticipation, no pleasure. She felt numb.

From the room behind her she heard Brad's voice speaking to the bellhop, but she didn't turn around. She had nothing to say to Brad at the moment. Only questions that needed to be asked eventually, and decisions to discuss. But even the answers to those ques-

tions could do little to change the present situation.
Nothing could change the fact that she was now offi-
cially on her honeymoon—with the wrong man.

Staring out at the panorama spread far below her,
Penny knew when Brad opened the wide sliding glass
door and joined her on the balcony. She didn't turn
around.

They had spoken very little since leaving the church.
By the time they made their connections and were on
the plane to Acapulco, Penny felt exhausted. She slept
most of the way.

Penny recognized Brad's dispirited mood and no
longer believed this was another one of his pranks.
During the reception, fleeting memories of their conversation the night before had occurred to her.

Penny realized that the blow to his head hadn't affected him as she had thought at the time. He'd been
trying to warn her that Gregory wasn't going to be at
the church. One of her questions was how he had
known. What could he have said or done to cause
Gregory to risk ruining his reputation in Payton rather
than marry her? Whatever it was, Penny knew she
wasn't quite ready to face Brad's possible treachery.

And that was the cruelest blow of all. That Brad,
her childhood friend, her most trusted companion,
could be responsible for what had happened.

If that were true, she had not only lost her fiancé but
her belief in the integrity of her best friend. How
ironic that she was now married to him.

"The view is really something, isn't it?" Brad said
quietly.

She could hear the tenseness in his voice. He wasn't feeling any better about the recent turn of events than she was. She supposed that was something they had in common at the moment.

"Yes."

When she didn't say anything more, he asked, "Are you hungry?"

"No."

"Neither am I." Brad pulled out one of the chairs tucked under a small table on the balcony and sat down. "At least we're away from the comments of all the well-wishers," he offered in a gentle voice. "Are you very tired?"

Penny continued to gaze out toward the beach. She hadn't looked at him since he'd joined her. Without turning she said, "Not really. I slept on the plane."

Brad was very aware of that. After she had fallen asleep he had pulled her into his arms so that she slept with her head on his shoulder. What had torn at his heart were the tears she had shed in her sleep.

Why had he ever thought that she would prefer to marry him than be abandoned at the church? Why had Gregory ever suggested it? Unconsciously he rubbed his head. Perhaps that was it—the blow to his head. His brains had been addled. Despite doing everything in his power to prevent it he had managed to hurt her, the very last thing he would ever have wanted.

Penny caught sight of the movement and turned slightly to see Brad massaging his forehead.

"Is your head bothering you?" she asked, suddenly remembering all that he had been through that week. She had been so wrapped up in her own misery she had forgotten what he was going through.

"A little."

"Why don't you take some pain medication and try to rest?"

He looked up at her and smiled ruefully. "Because the stuff is so strong, it puts me out for hours."

Penny found herself smiling for the first time since the wedding reception. "I don't find that such an unfavorable side effect. I wouldn't mind being unconscious for a while, myself."

His eyes met hers in total understanding. They had shared so much over the years. Today was one more experience that strengthened the bond between them. When the challenge of the reception confronted them, they had immediately united and faced the crisis together. Now that it was over, they could fall apart without fear of the other's ridicule.

Brad wondered if Penny had any idea how rare that bond was. Or if she cared.

"Good point," he said, answering her smile. "I may just take your advice." He glanced around, taking in the view from the balcony. "We certainly found a spectacular spot to hide and lick our wounds, wouldn't you say?"

She heard the underlying pain in his voice and she closed her eyes, almost wincing at the sound. Brad looked tired, as though he hadn't slept much in the past twenty-four hours.

His decision must have caused him a great deal of agony, and her accusations hadn't made the situation any easier. She had struck out at him in pain, perhaps unconsciously hoping to ease her own. Why had she placed all the blame on him?

Penny acknowledged that sometimes, when a person is so filled with hurt and the pain takes over, it's hard to recall who administered what particular jab of agony. She had struck out at Brad for some of the pain inflicted by Gregory.

"I'm sorry for all of those hateful things I said to you earlier," Penny said slowly, opening her eyes and meeting his gaze.

His gaze seemed to soften and grow warmer. "Thank you for that, Penny," he replied.

"I think everything will look a little better to us in a few days," Penny said, "once we've had a chance to get used to the idea of what has happened. We don't have to make any decisions today." She walked over to him and softly stroked his forehead. "Why don't you take something for that headache, okay?"

He studied the expression on her face for a long, silent moment. Apparently satisfied with what he saw, Brad nodded. "I think you're right. Without this throbbing in my head, I could probably think a lot more clearly."

Penny watched him walk back into their room. He took off his coat and tie, then opened his suitcase and took out the small bottle of tablets. After disappearing into the bathroom he soon reappeared, sat on the side of the bed and slipped off his shoes.

She could almost feel the groan of relief he gave when he stretched out on the bed and closed his eyes.

Poor Brad.

It was amazing how quickly her perspective changed as soon as she began to think of someone besides herself, Penny thought wryly. She had certainly been enjoying a pity party of her own all day—feeling misused, abused and totally duped.

She needed to look at what the nefarious Brad had done to her. Why, the dastardly fellow had sought her out the night before and attempted to explain that her fiancé had backed out of their engagement at the last minute. When she refused to take him seriously, Brad, being the blackguard he was, had filled in as bridegroom rather than leave her to face a crowded church alone.

Gregory was the one who needed to make explanations. Penny shook her head wearily. What difference did it make? It was much too late to search for answers, but she knew that her mind would busily work to solve the mystery of the disappearing bridegroom.

How well do we ever get to know a person? Penny wondered, leaning against the railing and looking toward the water. No matter how hard we try, there are too many depths to be plumbed in a person to hope that we can ever completely know him.

She probably knew Brad Crawford better than she knew any other living human being. He knew her equally well. He'd once mentioned to her that the knowledge they shared about each other was more significant than she had ever acknowledged.

One thing Penny knew with fierce certainty—Brad would never have done to her what Gregory had done. Never.

She sighed. Today had been the most traumatic day of her life. She was glad to see it end.

Penny slowly entered their room, unsurprised to find Brad asleep. A frown still creased his brow and without thought she reached over to smooth it away with her forefinger.

He muttered something and shifted restlessly on the bed. It sounded as though he had said "Penny." She felt an ache in her chest. It wouldn't be surprising if he were having nightmares with her in the starring role.

Poor Brad. When he had decided to go home to attend a friend's wedding, the last thing he'd expected was to find himself in a featured role.

Penny wandered into the bathroom, a little awed by the luxurious fixtures. "Well, Penny, old girl, it's your wedding night, so how do you intend to spend it?" She reached over and turned on the water in the large tub. A warm soak in the tub sounded like a good way to relax. Too bad she hadn't thought of bringing along a good book to read, she decided whimsically.

And then she'd probably be ready for bed. Bed. She was going to share her bed with Brad. Of course it wouldn't be the first time. But the last time they'd slept together was on a camping trip when the zipper wouldn't work on her sleeping bag and he had offered to share his. As she recalled, she was eight years old at the time.

Somehow she knew that sharing a bed with the adult Brad would be an entirely different experience.

Almost an hour passed before Penny decided that as enjoyable as the water was, there was only so much fun to be had soaking in a tub.

Why was she trying so hard not to think about what this night was supposed to have been? The sooner she came to grips with the reality of her life, and accepted it, the sooner she'd be able to put away her sorrow that the tapestry of dreams she'd woven over the past several months had come unraveled.

After drying herself, Penny remembered that her suitcase still waited to be unpacked. She wrapped the enormous towel around her and grinned. One advantage of being small was that it didn't take much to cover her. This particular towel hung below her knees.

Quietly opening the door she walked into the bedroom. Brad had rolled onto his side and his face had lost its grimness. He was well and truly asleep.

When Penny opened her suitcase she was forcibly reminded of her situation. Her bag was filled with the frothy lingerie and sleepwear she'd received from the numerous showers her friends had given for her. She remembered all the teasing and chuckles regarding the sheerness of the nightgowns and undergarments.

She suddenly yearned for one of her sturdy football jerseys that had kept her company for so many years. Too bad she hadn't had the foresight to pack at least one.

Eventually she found a peach satin gown that was more opaque than any of the others and took it back into the bathroom to put on. When she glanced into the mirror later she wondered why she had thought it would be less revealing.

The satin was cut on the bias and the gown was designed to look like an evening gown from the thirties. Thin straps widened to a well-cupped bodice. An insert of matching peach lace formed a diamond, with a point that nestled just below her breasts, widened at the waist, then made another point on her abdomen. When she moved, the satin slid over her body highlighting each curve and forming shadows at each indentation.

Glancing at her watch, Penny admitted to herself that she had stalled long enough. It was time to go to bed. Turning out the light in the bathroom, she entered the bedroom once again. Only one lamp was on and it was across the room from the bed. She hadn't wanted to wake Brad when she'd come in earlier to find something to sleep in.

She turned back the covers on one side of the bed, thankful of its extra width, then crossed the room and turned off the light. With the room darkened she was drawn to the lighter expanse of the glass door. She peered outside. The stars seemed so bright she felt she could almost reach up and touch one. Out at sea, she could spot an occasional flash of white where a wave had broken.

What a beautiful spot for a honeymoon.

She returned to the bed and carefully slid in. Oh, how wonderful to lie down at last, was her last conscious thought.

Moonlight pouring through the wide, uncurtained expanse of glass aroused Brad several hours later. He sat up, disoriented. Looking around him he suddenly remembered where he was. Damn! He'd done it again—fallen asleep for too many hours. Thoughtfully he touched his head. At least the headache was gone, he decided.

Penny was curled beside him, although she was underneath the covers. Gingerly he slid off the bed and stood while continuing to gaze at her. She looked so peaceful and serene.

Brad felt as if his heart would explode with the feeling that swelled up inside of him. He had never loved another person as much, and in so many ways, as he loved Penny Blackwell. Penny Crawford, he reminded himself. She was now his wife. His wife!

How many years had he dreamed about someday being married to Penny—making love to her, acting with her, raising children with her...teasing and laughing and enjoying life with her. When had that dream died?

He knew to the minute. The day he'd opened the mail in his New York apartment and found the invitation to her wedding.

He'd felt betrayed. How dare she! He'd been angry and hurt and felt deceived by those he'd most trusted.

All the time he'd been in New York he'd written to her, but Penny was the world's worst correspondent. Even when his mother had written that she was dating a lawyer, he hadn't been terribly concerned. He was dating, as well. Wasn't that the idea? For them to be sure how they felt?

He had been sure. He'd always known, from the time Penny had fallen out of a swing when she was four years old and he'd cried because she cried. He'd felt her pain. She was as much a part of him as his heart or lungs.

How could she possibly not love him in the same way? How could she not know how important they were to each other? The distance had never mattered to him because she had always been in his heart. He could call her up in his mind at will.

He'd studied the invitation and begun to plot. He would go home and put a stop to the whole thing—make her admit that she couldn't possibly love anyone else—that the two of them belonged together.

However, things hadn't quite worked out that way for him. In the first place, he was under contract and couldn't just take off. But he'd started talking to anyone who would listen. He needed some time off. There was a family crisis, one that needed his presence.

Eventually the powers that be had considered the possibility. Then they had needed to prepare new story lines, and that took time, and more time. Only time was quickly running out for Brad.

He'd ended up with a week. One lousy week to try to convince her she was marrying the wrong man. He'd realized as soon as he saw her that his task was going to be tougher than he'd expected.

Penny had changed from the woman he knew so well. That was when he had finally given up hope. He realized he could never do anything that would hurt her, and breaking up an engagement a week before the wedding was inexcusable. He loved her enough to let her go, knowing that nothing in his life would ever be quite so wonderful or joyous or sparkling again. Losing Penny was like losing all the sparkle in champagne. Life would be flat without her.

Somehow he should have known that life would never betray him in such a cold, calculating way. He'd been given another chance to win.

Looking down at her now, he realized he still had a considerable way to go to win her. But what better setting, or more romantic place, could there be to woo the woman that was already his wife?

Brad walked into the bathroom and shut the door. Turning on the shower he adjusted the heat of the water, stripped down and stepped under the invigorating spray.

Did Penny really love him enough to want to continue their marriage? She had told him she loved him, but what did she actually feel? How did a person ever know what another was feeling? Each person had his own conception of what love was, what it felt like, and how he responded to it.

Somehow he had to prove to Penny, as well as to himself, that she loved him and that marrying Brad, instead of Gregory, was the best thing that could have happened to her.

Brad was convinced he wouldn't be able to go back to sleep, not with all he had on his mind, and not with Penny lying so close beside him. He was unaware how quickly he fell asleep after he joined Penny in bed, this time under the covers.

Penny's dream carried her along on a wave of pleasure that she had never before experienced. She was on the boat, out on the lake, and she could feel the warm sunshine and a soft breeze. Brad was there, fussing because she hadn't put on more suntan lotion and insisting she would burn without it.

He was such a nag. She handed him the lotion and suggested that he put it on himself if he didn't like the way she did it. He grinned at her and she could no longer be irritated with him.

Brad began to spread the cream along her back with long, exploring strokes. She loved his touch. He was so gentle and yet his hands were strong, his long fingers sensitive. She could feel the pads of his fingertips softly moving over her.

She shifted to give him better access to her body, wanting him to continue touching her. He responded by sliding his hand from her back, along her arm, down to her waist, then up once again. Those sensitive fingertips lightly drew a line beneath her breasts and Penny wished he wouldn't tease her so. She wanted to feel his hands touching her—Aahh. He cupped her breast with his hand and she was pleased how well it fit his hand. Once again his fingertips caressed her, this time they rubbed gently, back and forth, across her nipple. She thought she would cry out at the unexpected pleasure of his touch.

No man had ever touched her so intimately. Only Brad. She loved Brad, so it was all right. Whatever Brad wanted to do, it was all right. She loved him. She loved . . .

Penny's eyes flew open. She was no longer asleep. No longer dreaming, and yet—she was in Brad's arms.

Her head lay on his shoulder, his arm holding her close to his side. And with his other hand, he was touching and caressing her. And she was letting him.

Her breasts ached with the fullness that his fingers had encouraged. Penny became aware that her legs were intertwined with his, his thigh was nestled between hers. It was as though their bodies knew better than their minds how comfortably they fit together.

Brad shifted, pulling her tighter against him, lifting her chin as he lowered his head to hers. She barely had time to notice that his eyes were closed before his lips touched hers and she forgot everything else.

He was kissing her in the same way he had at the reception, but with even more intimacy. Penny felt devoured. His tongue took possession of her mouth as if by right. He continued to softly brush his hand back and forth across the crest of her breast and Penny felt as though all of her insides were melting.

New sensations shot through her and she became aware of parts of her body that had never drawn her attention before. Her hand seemed to have developed a will of its own and she began to move it over his chest, reveling in the way the rough texture of his chest felt against her palm.

She could feel the heavy vibration of his heart pounding against her. His lungs seemed to be laboring for air but he continued to kiss her without pausing for breath.

Penny was only fleetingly aware that he was sliding the thin strap of her gown off her shoulder. She couldn't find the energy to either help or resist. The dreamlike state she'd been in seemed to continue.

"Oh, Penny," he managed to say when he finally broke away. His breathing was so ragged she could scarcely hear him. "I want you so much," he murmured. "So much."

She didn't need his explanation to know what was happening. Somehow everything that was occurring seemed so natural and right.

Both of them were still more than half-asleep, uninhibitedly responding to their deep-seated, longstanding feelings for each other.

Vaguely Brad knew that he intended to make love to Penny. He loved her, they were married, and he knew of no better way to convince her that he wanted nothing more than to be her passionately loving husband.

But when he stroked his fingers over her abdomen and down, he felt her body stiffen and he paused.

Brad knew he could seduce her. From her reactions he realized she'd never been this aroused before. He knew she wouldn't stop him, if he took his time with her.

The question was, how was she going to feel afterward? There was so much that needed to be said between them. Even though they were legally married, the wedding had been a farce.

Did he really intend to use her sexual response to him to coax her into making a decision that would have lifelong ramifications for both of them?

Brad relaxed his hold on her and lay there, unmoving for a moment.

Penny felt swamped with all of the swirling, unfamiliar emotions she'd been experiencing since she'd awakened. Everything was happening so fast. Her lifelong friend had metamorphosed into a passionate, intriguing stranger whose very touch made her bones melt.

Before she could fully comprehend what was happening, Penny felt Brad move away from her. She watched with bewilderment as Brad tossed the covers back and, clad only in a pair of briefs, disappeared into the bathroom, closing the door behind him.

Chapter Nine

When the bathroom door opened sometime later Brad walked out and casually commented. "I'm sorry I took so long. I guess we'll have to flip a coin each morning to see who gets the use of the bathroom first."

This was the same Brad she'd always known, but Penny discovered she missed the passionate stranger who had shared her bed. She wondered what he would think if he knew how she felt. "That's all right," she said, following his example and entering the other room.

Brad quickly found some clean clothes and, dropping the towel he'd draped modestly around him, got dressed. She won't have any problem with the hot water, he thought wryly. I certainly didn't use much of it.

He was waiting for her when she came out, wrapped in a towel. "I'm sorry about what almost happened this morning," he said tersely. "I have no excuse for losing control like that. I hope you won't add this to the long list you seem to have kept over the years of my iniquities."

Brad stood by the opened door to their balcony, waiting for her reaction. She could think of nothing to say.

"We need to talk, Penny, the sooner the better. I've discovered I'm not nearly as noble as I thought I was."

After what she had just experienced with him, Penny wasn't at all sure she wanted his nobility. She'd made an astounding discovery since he'd disappeared into the bathroom earlier.

She very much wanted to make love to Brad Crawford. The thought shocked her right down to her toes. If that was what she was feeling for Brad, she'd had no business planning to marry Gregory Duncan.

Another revelation.

She was still reeling from these shocks when Brad greeted her with his apology in a no-nonsense tone of voice. Glancing down at her towel-draped body, she said, "I agree that we need to talk. I'd prefer to be dressed to do it, however."

Brad seemed to find her remark amusing. "I suppose I can understand that. Why don't you go ahead and get ready and I'll meet you downstairs for breakfast. Maybe later we can take a walk along the beach and enjoy some of the atmosphere around here."

"All right." Penny still felt bewildered by her responses to him earlier and her illuminating discovery regarding her feelings for Brad.

She wasted little time finding a sundress to put on, pleased that so much of what she had packed would be appropriate for a honeymoon in Acapulco.

Her honeymoon with Brad.

A conversation she'd had with her mother months ago suddenly flashed into her mind. She had told Helen that Gregory had proposed to her.

Helen had been working in the kitchen at the time so Penny had perched on the step stool nearby.

"Gregory wants to marry you!" Helen repeated in obvious surprise.

"That's what he said," Penny agreed.

"What did you tell him?"

Penny was quiet for a moment. "I told him that I needed time to consider it."

"I should think so!"

"However, I'm fairly sure that I want to marry him, Mom."

Helen turned around and faced her. "Are you, Penny?"

Penny met her mother's look and nodded. "Yes. Gregory offers the type of life I want. He's stable, successful and I know I can always depend on him."

"What about love?"

"That goes without saying, of course."

"Love should never go without being expressed, Penny. Don't mistake compatible and companionable with love. They're necessary to a good relationship, but love is what holds them together."

"I think we're well-suited."

Helen sighed. "I always thought you and Brad would end up together."

"Brad? You must be joking. That man wouldn't know the first thing about making a commitment. He'd run in the opposite direction."

The image of her mother's face dissolved and once again Penny realized where she was—on her honeymoon with Brad.

He'd had every opportunity to run—from the time he'd learned that Gregory wasn't going to marry her— to the day of the wedding and afterward. But he was here. Despite the disruption a sudden marriage would cause in his life and career, Brad Crawford had chosen to commit himself to her and face whatever consequences his actions created.

When Penny returned to the bathroom to put on her makeup she was arrested by the sight of the woman in the mirror. She glowed. There was no other word to describe the look of anticipation on her face. She was a woman in love, there was no denying that expression, the sparkle in her eyes, the slight flush to her cheeks.

Penny couldn't remember the last time she'd faced that woman in a mirror. Gone was the sedate school teacher, the level-headed, sensible woman Gregory Duncan had met and asked to marry. Instead she saw the young girl she'd known years ago, her dreams and fantasies shining like an aura around her.

"I had no idea you even existed," she whispered. Why had she brushed aside this vibrant person who had patiently waited to be recognized? Why had she felt the need to deny the spontaneity that seemed to bubble inside of her?

Here was the woman who had loved Brad Crawford single-mindedly, had followed his lead throughout her childhood, and had played opposite him in most of the plays produced during their high school and college years.

"Where have you been?" she asked, amazed at the transformation.

From the moment she had awakened in Brad's arms to the feel of his touch and the taste of his lips, Penny felt like an entirely different person. She was reminded of one of her favorite stories as a child—the one about Sleeping Beauty, who was awakened by the prince with a kiss.

Her pulse accelerated at the thought that she could have married Gregory, convinced that she loved him, and never known the wonder of what Brad had already revealed to her. She had never been affected by Gregory in such a way. Penny had never known the difference . . . until now.

She laughed out loud, hurriedly finished applying her lipstick and flicked a comb through her hair. How could she explain what had happened to her when she didn't understand it herself? She cringed with embarrassment at the memory of all that she had accused Brad of the day before. He could have reacted so differently. Gregory would never have tolerated such an outburst from her. Subconsciously she had known that her innermost personality must be kept submerged in order to be acceptable to him.

With Brad, she'd always done and said exactly what she felt at the time. He was so much a part of her that she had never questioned that particular freedom. Nor had she fully appreciated it.

Now he waited for her downstairs, no doubt expecting another childish outburst. His list of iniquities? How about hers? To think that he loved her, despite all her faults. It was up to her to let him know that, for the first time, she fully realized how much he meant to her.

Penny rode the elevator down to the main floor of the hotel, unaware of the smile on her face. Brad noticed her expression as soon as she stepped into the lobby.

"I've seen that particular smile before," he said in a low voice, taking her arm and guiding her into the restaurant. "It bodes ill to someone."

She shook her head. "Not necessarily."

After they were seated and their coffee was poured, he leaned forward slightly and said, "For someone whose life was ruined yesterday, you seem to have made an amazing recovery."

She chuckled, amused by the wariness on his face, "What a difference a day makes, wouldn't you say?"

"That isn't something I find myself muttering very often, as a matter of fact. Actually, you're beginning to make me nervous."

"In what way?"

"I can recall several instances where that particular look in your eye meant trouble for me."

She shook her head with a grin.

"I've got it. You're leaving right after breakfast, flying back home."

"Nope."

"You've made arrangements to rendezvous with a local skin diver?"

She laughed outright. "Don't be silly."

He leaned back and studied her intently. "Oh. Now understand. You've heard from Gregory."

She sobered. "Why would you say that?"

He shrugged. "Because you look so radiant. Somehow he must have let you know he's sorry and intends to make amends."

"Brad, I haven't heard from Gregory. It wouldn't matter if I had."

"What's that supposed to mean?"

She glanced up as the waiter delivered their breakfast. "Hmm. Doesn't that look wonderful? I can't remember when I've been so hungry, can you?"

For the rest of the meal Penny adroitly avoided anything resembling a serious conversation. She wanted to enjoy these new sensations she'd discovered and to come to terms with the insight she'd gained about herself.

She wondered if this was how a butterfly felt when it first opened its wings—astounded at the myriad of bright colors unfolding. Suddenly she felt free of the restrictions that she'd unknowingly placed on herself.

Today was a brand-new day for her to face the world and adjust to her new life and the person she'd just discovered.

Thank God Brad was a part of her new existence. He was a major part.

They had walked along the beach for some time in silence, watching the swimmers playing in the surf. Finally Brad said, "You're taking this much better than I expected."

"I've had time to think it over."

"And?"

"And what?"

"Have you come to any conclusions as to what you want to do?"

"About what?"

"Us. Our marriage."

He'd been quiet during most of their walk on the beach and she'd known he was thinking. "Some. What about you?" she asked.

"Well," he said after a moment, "I know that I really managed to mess up your life by trying to help out."

"Oh?"

"You might have gone through a few bad days, trying to face everyone when the wedding had to be called off, but then it would have been over, and you could have gone on with your life."

"Yes, I've thought of that."

"Instead, you're now going to have to..." He paused, as though unsure of what to say.

"I'm going to have to... what?"

"You're still going to have to explain why you ended your marriage so quickly."

"You do have a point there. How do we return home and tell everyone that we flunked our honeymoon?"

His head snapped around and he stared at her in surprise. She had an amused expression that added lightness to her teasing comment.

"I think we have our roles reversed here, don't you?" he finally muttered. "I'm the one you're always accusing of never taking anything seriously."

"Yes, that's true. I decided to see if I could become more like you. You've set such an example all these years."

"This isn't exactly the subject I'd use to practice my sense of humor, Penny."

"I don't see why not to use it. The fact is, we are married. To each other. I am very much aware that your vacation plans did not include acquiring a wife. But try to overlook that particular inconvenience and see if you can enjoy your time here," she said, waving her arms at the water, the palm trees and the carefully groomed sand.

Brad had never seen Penny in quite this mood before. Maybe the strain had been too much for her and her nerves had finally snapped. He'd find it difficult to convince anyone of that, however. She looked radiantly healthy and happy. And in love.

Whoa! Wait a minute. That line of thinking was going to get him in trouble. "Are you suggesting we postpone for a few days deciding what we're going to do when we return to the States?"

"Is there anything wrong with that?" she asked.

Brad thought of the long cold shower he'd endured that morning and almost shuddered. What she suggested wasn't unfair, just humanly impossible for him. Wasn't she affected by sharing a room with him, a bed with him? Hadn't their early morning kiss and caresses warned her of what could happen if they continued to ignore what was between them?

"I don't suppose there is," he finally answered.

"Good," she said, stopping and looking out at the water. "We've waited long enough after breakfast for a swim, don't you think?" she asked.

He glanced at his watch. "Yes."

"Then let's go change into our suits. I can hardly wait to find out what it's like to swim in sea water."

For the next several hours they kept busy, first swimming, then exploring the area, and finally spending a romantic evening watching the divers go off the cliff into the sea below.

Brad had forced himself not to dwell on the night ahead, but as the evening progressed, he had a hard time disciplining himself. He'd never seen Penny more beautiful, enticing, alluring, and yet so unobtainable.

This was his punishment for his sin of coveting her. She was his wife, but he was honor bound not to presume anything regarding their relationship.

By the time they returned to their room, he'd almost decided to fake another headache as an excuse to take more pain medication. At least he could seek oblivion for a few hours.

Penny gathered up her nightclothes and went into the bathroom. She smiled and said, "I won't be long."

"That's what I'm afraid of," he muttered to himself wondering at his unusual ability to inflict pain upon himself. Wandering out on the balcony he studied the stars and tried to imagine where he would be if the wedding had gone as originally planned.

He felt a gut-wrenching pain at the thought of Penny here with anyone else but him. How could he possibly have borne it, knowing he'd never share this delightful intimacy with her? If that's the case, he thought, then you'd better convince her that the two of you belong together.

To his amazement Brad discovered a few minutes later that he needed to make very little effort.

He turned when he heard the door open and saw her standing there in a thin gown that left very little to the imagination, particularly as she was silhouetted against the bathroom light.

"Penny..." he said, trying to get his tongue unwrapped from around his teeth.

She walked over to him and casually put her hand on his chest. "Thank you for your patience."

There was something in her tone of voice that made him believe she was referring to something other than her use of the bathroom.

Brad could no more stand there and not touch her than he could leap from the balcony and fly. "That's okay. I, uh, think maybe that I'll..."

Penny went up on tiptoe and kissed him softly on the lips, her body relaxing fully against him. If his mind was attempting to resist what was happening, his body obviously did not suffer from similar scruples. It immediately responded to her closeness.

Instead of being repelled, Penny cuddled even closer, if that were possible.

The battle within Brad was intense but short-lived. He might hate himself in the morning, but there was no resisting what he felt tonight.

Penny knew exactly when Brad stopped fighting and gave free rein to what they both wanted to happen. His arms came around her in a grip so fierce she had a fleeting thought as to the safety of her ribs. But it was only a fleeting thought, after all. Having Brad hold her so fiercely was well worth any damage she might accidently suffer.

The kiss he gave her held all the longing that she could possibly want from him and when he paused a moment for them to get their breath she whispered, "Love me, Brad. Please love me."

"Oh, God, Penny. Don't you understand how much I love you?"

"Then show me."

He needed no further encouragment. Brad lifted her in his arms and strode over to the bed. Brushing the covers back, he lowered her onto the pillow.

Brad impatiently stripped out of his clothes, then came down onto the bed beside her. "Oh, love," he muttered as he gathered her in his arms. "Do you have any idea what you've put me through?"

"Not intentionally, Brad. I didn't know," she whispered. "How could I have known?"

Eventually he removed the gown she wore for the express purpose of getting his attention. Penny was more than satisfied with the results.

Brad took his time now that he had accepted the amazing fact that Penny wanted him and was willing to explore the physical side of their multi-faceted relationship.

She willingly followed his silent guidance, imitating each caress. Penny was delighted to see his immediate response to her touch.

By the time he was ready to claim her, she was almost pleading with him to show her the next step in their lovemaking. Yet nothing could have possibly described how wonderful she felt when Brad finally made her his own.

How could they have waited so long to experience something so beautiful, so fulfilling? If only she had known what she had been missing.

And later, just before she drifted off to sleep, Penny reminded herself to ask Brad where he'd learned to be such a gentle, sensitive, and obviously experienced lover!

They slept late the next morning, content to use the morning hours to catch up on sleep that had been abandoned willingly more than once during the night.

Penny quickly became adept at learning Brad's most vulnerable places. She discovered a great many advantages to knowing a person so well. Sharing a marriage bed became something of an adventure.

Until now, Penny had assumed she was not a particularly sensual individual. In a few short hours, she learned differently.

When she eventually awoke the next morning she saw that Brad was still sleeping. However, since he had an arm and a leg wrapped around her, she realized she wasn't going anywhere until he moved.

"Brad?" she whispered.

"Good grief, Penny," he mumbled. "You're insatiable." His mouth quirked into a mischievous grin.

"Would you kindly let go of me?"

His eyes flew open at her tone. "What's wrong?" he asked with a sinking feeling in the pit of his stomach.

She waited until he edged away from her, then she sat up with a grin. "Nothing. I just have to answer nature's call." Penny fled to the bathroom, laughing, the pillow that followed her barely missing its target.

He lay there for a moment, thinking about the previous night. If Penny intended to dissolve their marriage, she certainly couldn't ask for an annulment. Somehow he doubted her interest in pursuing such a course of action, if her response to him the night before was any indication.

When Brad heard the shower running, he decided to join her.

"What are you doing?" Her startled cry greeted him when he stepped into the shower with her.

"What does it look like?"

"I thought we were going to take turns," she said, suddenly shy with him.

He took the soap from her hand and began to apply it lavishly over her body. "But this is so much more economical, don't you think? We'll be able to get ready that much faster, and look at the water we're saving."

Penny could find nothing to say to refute his statement, so she smiled.

"We still need to talk, you know," he said quietly, after lovingly caressing her all over, then carefully rinsing her off.

"I know."

Penny felt much better prepared to discuss their future together after the night they had just spent. They belonged together, even if they had chosen a rather unorthodox way to achieve that goal. Or to be more precise, *he* had chosen.

They chose to order breakfast sent up so they could enjoy the view from their balcony and not have to dress any more than was necessary to greet the man who delivered their order.

"Are you coming back to New York with me?" Brad finally asked her over coffee.

"I suppose. I guess I haven't really thought about it."

"That's understandable, under the circumstances."

"I really have no desire to stay in Payton. I'm not ready to face Gregory just yet."

Brad could feel his stomach clench at the mention of the other man's name. He took another sip of coffee, not meeting her eyes. "I have to go back on Sunday to be ready to work Monday."

"It seems so strange to be planning to live in New York. Like another world. I'll need to resign my job..." Her voice trailed off.

"You know you don't need to work if you'd rather not," he offered.

"I'd go crazy sitting around all day."

"That's not what I meant. Since we don't need your income, you could take the opportunity to attend auditions and things . . . if you wanted to, of course."

"You mean, try to get a job acting?"

"You've certainly got the credentials for it."

"Oh, Brad, I don't know."

"About what?"

"I just never thought I'd try to act professionally."

He smiled. "Try it. You might decide you like it."

So many things were happening to her in a space of a few days, Penny felt as though a whirlwind had picked her up and swirled her away to another land. A land of endless possibilities.

She gazed at Brad across the table. He looked very relaxed and contented. She couldn't imagine Gregory sitting spinelessly in a chair, with nothing more on than a pair of swimming trunks. They were so different and yet she had been attracted to the one she had felt was more stable.

Her instincts had failed her. But Brad hadn't. She remembered the phrase he'd repeated to her—that's what friends are for.

"Thank you," Penny said with a tender look on her face.

Since Brad couldn't remember anything he'd done that deserved such a comment, he looked at her blankly.

She explained. "Thank you for loving me, for having faith in me, for pushing me until I had to face myself and learn who I really am. I realize now that I would have been miserably bored with Gregory.

Thank you for understanding that and doing what you could to save me from my own faulty decisions.''

Brad straightened in his chair and stared at her with a look that seemed to radiate happiness. ''You mean you're forgiving me for ruining your wedding?''

''You didn't ruin it. You saved it and me.''

''I know you still love Gregory, Penny. I can understand and live with that . . .''

She laughed. ''I've never heard you sounding so humble, Brad. And it doesn't go with your personality at all. I'm not sure how I feel toward Gregory at the moment. What he did was brutal and inexcusable. Learning that he was capable of such behavior shocked me, because I realized how little I knew him. I'm immensely thankful I didn't marry him.'' She gazed out over the water. ''It never would have worked for us.''

''I was very much afraid you'd never see that,'' Brad said with relief.

Penny got up and trailed around to Brad's side of the table. She sat down on his lap and looked up at him. ''There is one thing I have wanted to ask you, though.''

Brad tensed. Things were going so well. They hadn't fought since their wedding day. Of course, that had only been two days ago, but he felt they'd made giant strides in learning to live together compatibly.

''What?'' he asked warily.

''I've known you all your life,'' she began softly.

''That's right,'' he agreed.

''We were always very close, except for those three years you were in New York,'' she went on.

"Uh-huh."

"Then could you explain how you perfected your technique in bed? I seem to have missed something along the way."

Brad tilted his head back and laughed. Still laughing he picked her up and carried her back into the other room. Since she wore only a negligee that did little to cover her charms, he wasted no time in freeing her of her apparel.

As he lowered her to the bed and stretched out beside her, he said, "Honey, you haven't missed a thing. I intend to teach you all that I know. I told you that not all I learned in college was in the classroom."

There was that devastating grin again, the one that caused women all over America to turn on their television sets every afternoon.

The love in his eyes made it clear that there was only one woman who had his heart. She held him closely, thankful for the chance she'd had to discover just what friends are for.

Epilogue

Hello," the young secretary said with a smile. "May I help you?"

"I would like to see Mr. Duncan, if possible."

"Do you have an appointment?"

"No, I'm afraid I don't."

The secretary nodded. "I'll see if he has time to see you. Your name, please?"

"Penny Crawford," she said quietly.

While the young woman spoke on the phone, Penny looked around the office. Not much had changed since the last time she'd been there. Everything had a stately, polished look that induced a sense of reassurance and stability.

She heard a door open behind her and she turned around. Gregory Duncan stood in the doorway, staring at her. "Penny! I thought she must have misunderstood—Come in," he said, stepping aside and motioning her into his office.

Penny walked past him, noticing the changes in him since she'd seen him last. He looked older, which she had expected, but much older than his years. Lines furrowed his brow and face. Up close she could see the gray in his blond hair. He looked just what he was—a successful, harried businessman. She wondered what she'd ever seen in him that she'd found attractive. The physical resemblance between Gregory and Brad was barely discernible.

"This is a surprise," he said from behind her. "Won't you have a seat?"

"I hope you don't mind my dropping in like this," she said, taking a seat and watching him as he walked behind his desk and sat down.

"Why, no. It's a pleasure to see you again. It's been a while."

Her eyes met his. "Yes, it has," she agreed quietly.

They sat there in silence, just looking at each other. Finally Gregory roused himself enough to say, "You're looking wonderful."

She nodded her head. "Thank you."

"Are you in town for long?"

"Just a few days, I'm afraid. We don't get much free time these days."

He smiled. "I suppose not. How does it feel to be working with your husband on stage?"

"It's been quite an experience. Surprisingly enough, Brad enjoys it. I was afraid television had spoiled him for the theater."

"Your reviews have been very good."

"Yes." She paused, searching for the right words. "I wanted to thank you for the beautiful bouquet you had delivered to me on opening night." Once more her eyes met his. "I was touched that you remembered me."

"I will always remember you, Penny," he said in a matter-of-fact tone. "As a matter of fact, I was in New York and caught your opening night."

"You were there?"

He nodded.

"Then why didn't you come backstage?"

"I had intended to. But somehow, when the time came, it seemed inappropriate." He smiled again. "However, I thought you did an outstanding job, for what it's worth. I had no idea you were so talented."

"There was a lot of luck involved there. A case of being in the right place at the right time." She shrugged. "I wish you'd let me know you were there."

"There was no need. Let's say I was appeasing my curiosity." He nodded slightly. "You and Brad work very well together, you know. You seem to be so in tune with each other that the audience can almost see the link."

"I know. We've often remarked on it ourselves."

Gregory picked up a letter opener and began to turn it over, end to end, in his hands. "I suppose your families are pleased to see you," he said.

"Yes. Brad's mother hasn't been well. We thought she might enjoy seeing Stacye, but to be on the safe side, we decided to stay at Mother's. Stacye's energy can wear anyone out. We didn't think Brad's mom needed the extra strain. This way we can let her visit in small doses.''

"Do you have any pictures of her?" he asked casually.

Penny laughed. "Of course. I'm a typical doting mother." She dug around in her purse, then pulled out a folder and handed it to him.

Gregory studied the little girl carefully, noting the blond hair and the blue eyes. The smile was very familiar, as was the impish expression. It was her mother's smile, although he had never been exposed to the impish part of her personality.

"She looks a great deal like you, Penny," he said, handing the folder back to her.

"I suppose so. But she has her father's teasing temperament. Those two are a pair." She stopped suddenly, realizing what she was saying, and to whom.

"I don't need to ask if you're happy, Penny. It shows."

"I know, Gregory. That's why I came by to see you." His eyebrow lifted slightly in inquiry. "It took me a while," she went on to say, "but I finally understood what you did and why you did it."

He looked puzzled. "I'm afraid I don't follow you."

"I couldn't understand why you'd refuse to marry me without offering me any explanation, and yet present us with a honeymoon already paid for. On the one hand, one action was brutal, the other sensitive. The two actions didn't fit."

"I'm afraid you're being too generous in ascribing such kind motives to me, Penny," he said. "The truth

s that when it came right down to it, I realized I'd
been single too long, was too set in my ways to ever
accommodate another person in my life. And you
were right. I chose a brutal, cowardly way out." He
looked down at the letter opener in his hand, as
though wondering where it had come from. "As for
the honeymoon, I had paid for everything several
weeks in advance and would not have gotten the full
amount back, even if I'd canceled." His smile was a
little forced. "I'm afraid the tickets were a sop to my
conscience. Nothing more."

She could feel his embarrassment at being confronted by what he had done. Penny realized that she
believed him. He hadn't particularly cared about her
feelings, because emotions weren't very high on his list
of desirable qualities in himself. He was a practical,
pragmatic man. Had she married him, her own emotions would have eventually atrophied from lack of
expression.

"Well," she said, coming to her feet, "I wanted to
stop by and thank you for the flowers and your good
wishes, and to let you know that, just in case you've
wondered, you did the right thing when you refused to
marry me."

He stood as well. "I've never had any doubts about
that," he said with a small smile. He walked around
the desk and escorted her to the door. "Thank you for
coming in, Penny. I appreciate the gesture."

"Yes, I'm sure by this time tomorrow everyone in
town will know I came to see you," she replied with a
grin.

His smile was more natural when he said, "I don't know what story you and Brad put about, but I was inundated with unspoken sympathy for weeks after the wedding. Totally undeserved, of course. I felt like something of a fraud."

She laughed. "Since Brad engineered the whole scenario, he was responsible for the story. I didn't know who I was marrying until mid-way through the ceremony."

For once Gregory's face registered emotion. "You mean you didn't know that I wasn't...'" He couldn't seem to find the words.

"That's right," she said matter-of-factly. "Brad was convinced I would never have married him any other way."

"I had no idea."

She shrugged. "Well, that's Brad. Always being dramatic about something or other. Only the three of us know what actually happened. There was no reason for anyone else to know."

He stood there looking down at her for a long time in silence. Penny didn't feel as if she could turn and walk away from such an intent look.

"Brad must have known the best way to handle you," he said finally, still a little bemused.

"Yes, I guess he does. He's had enough practice." On impulse Penny went up on her toes and kissed his cheek. "Thank you for seeing me, Gregory. I always felt that our relationship had been left hanging, somehow. I needed to tie it off in my mind—to let you know that I've forgiven you for what you did. You did us both a real favor."

Penny's last sight of Gregory was his turning back to his office and his work—his real wife.

When Penny pulled into her parents' driveway, she saw Brad loping toward her from his parents' home. She got out and started toward him. He grabbed her around the waist, his momentum swinging her around.

"What are you doing, you crazy man?" she asked, laughing.

"I missed you. I was coming over to see if your Mother might have left a note that she had heard from you. Where have you been?"

They stood in the middle of the front lawn, their arms companionably wrapped around each other's waist. "I stopped in to see Gregory."

Brad's smile faded slowly. "Why?"

"It's hard to explain. Every once in a while I'd find myself thinking of him, what he was doing, if he'd ever married—that sort of thing."

"Wishing that things had turned out differently?" he asked with a smile. Penny was aware his eyes remained serious.

She went up on tiptoe and kissed him. "Hardly," she said with a grin, "I suppose I needed to see him again, in his own environment, to remind myself how close I came to making the biggest mistake of my life."

He held her close. "Was he surprised to see you?"

"Stunned is a better description. I don't think he ever thought he'd have to face me after what he did."

"So what did he say?"

"Not much. He saw the play the last time he was in New York. Seemed surprised that I could act."

Brad laughed. "He shouldn't have been surprised at all. You were giving him a great performance during your entire engagement."

Penny playfully poked him in the chest. "Not deliberately."

"I know, love," he said soothingly. Now his eyes were filled with mischief.

Brad turned toward the house and wrapped his arm around her shoulders. He glanced down at her with a grin. "Mom asked if Stacye could spend the afternoon with her. They're busy making cookies, so I said I thought it would be okay."

"Are you sure your mom's up to having such a little chatterbox around?"

He opened the door for them, then guided her up the stairs.

"Oh, I think so. She said the doctor thinks she's well on the road to recovery and that having her one and only granddaughter here was better than anything he could have prescribed." They reached the door to Penny's old room and Brad eased her inside, closing the door unobtrusively.

"Your mom went to town for her art class," he explained. "Said since she'd be late getting home we'd go out for dinner tonight." Brad casually began to unbutton Penny's dress.

"What are you doing?" she asked, suddenly aware of his preoccupation with her clothing.

He pushed her dress off her shoulders and eased it away from her breasts and rounded hips. "I'm rehearsing for a new role," he said with a grin, lifting

her and placing her on the bed. Brad quickly discarded his clothes and joined her.

"A new role?" she asked, a little breathless at the
sudden turn of events.

"Umm. Isn't this the way to play doctor?"

"I certainly hope not!" she said, looking at his un-
clothed body with feigned indignation.

"Oh, well. Maybe I just need some tender, loving
care, after an afternoon away from you."

She smiled, pulling him closer. "Well, my dear, you
certainly came to the right place for that."

"I know," Brad said with a satisfied smile.

*   *   *   *   *

ATTRACTIVE, SPACE SAVING
BOOK RACK

Display your most prized novels on this handsome and
sturdy book rack. The hand-rubbed walnut finish will
blend into your library decor with quiet elegance, providing a practical organizer for your favorite hard-or soft
covered books.

Only
$9.95

Approximately
16" x
when assembled

Assembles in seconds

To order, rush your name, address and zip code, along
with a check or money order for $10.70* ($9.95 plus 75¢
postage and handling) payable to *Silhouette Books*.

Silhouette Books
Book Rack Offer
901 Fuhrmann Blvd.
P.O. Box 1396
Buffalo, NY 14269-1396

Offer not available in Canada.

*New York and Iowa residents add appropriate sales tax.

COMING NEXT MONTH

**In response
to last year's outstanding success,
Silhouette Brings You:**

Silhouette Christmas Stories 1987

Specially chosen for you in a delightful volume celebrating the holiday season, four original romantic stories written by four of your favorite Silhouette authors.

Dixie Browning—*Henry the Ninth*
Ginna Gray—*Season of Miracles*
Linda Howard—*Bluebird Winter*
Diana Palmer—*The Humbug Man*

Each of these bestselling authors will enchant you with their unforgettable stories, exuding the magic of Christmas and the wonder of falling in love.

A heartwarming Christmas gift during the holiday season...indulge yourself and give this book to a special friend!

Available now

XM87-